EAGLE EYE

ALSO BY HORTENSE CALISHER

In the Absence of Angels
False Entry
Tale for the Mirror
Textures of Life
Extreme Magic
Journal from Ellipsia
The Railway Police and The Last Trolley Ride
The New Yorkers
Queenie
Herself
Standard Dreaming

EAGLE EYE

Hortense Calisher

ARBOR HOUSE

NEW YORK

Library of Congress Catalog Card No. 73–82181
ISBN 0‡87795–062–8
Manufactured in the United States of America

EAGLE   EYE

DID WEATHER EXIST, WHEN NOBODY LOOKED AT IT? Did it know? At dawn, say, on a summer Sunday in the financial district, in a suite on the forty-first floor? Whose only occupants were the owner, minimally sleeping in his windowless private eyrie at the center of it, and his son here in the outer office, lying naked and face down on a rug in front of a computer panel, not yet cracking an eye.

He lay doggo. Waking alone, he had wondered this in many far places, open fields and hostels, monasteries with a total glare of the sea, and one country divan some fifty miles out of New Delhi, where he had been fanned back to a consciousness that others too were supporting the weather, by a small child, with brows knitted in concern, and a Raphael mouth. But this day was the farthest of all.

9

Eagle Eye

Today we begin sweating out the world. Bronstein.

On the floor near his head lay all he possessed in it, boots and buckskins, a duffel-bag, and a jacket that by now was both tent and skin.

He reached out and patted the computer wall. The one at school, grubbed with handprints, was never like this. Morning, Batface. Remember a guy named Betts? He named you. Or the likes of you. We three worked together once. Please remember him.

And remember Bronstein. Both of you.

He pressed his face into the rug again. He still had the kind of red hair that made him a fact in other peoples' eyes, and the kind of stutter nobody notices. But his own eyes saw so much of late there must be something wrong with them.

Yesterday he'd had a twenty-first birthday party. A year late, but it should last him a lifetime. Both his parents, who gave it, were still around. Though since yesterday, his father, whom he'll see shortly, has the look of a man recently dead. And his mother, whom he suspects he will not see, already the nimbus of the far-distant but recently alive. Beyond that, archives of girls since he was thirteen, but no permanent one. They float through his time like tough ghosts. One in particular, trawling the catchwords he used to grab her for. Pastimes. Past time.

Tell me something, Batface. Are there still gentle friends to go to? Or must I put in more time learning what's worth murdering for?

Where do the people go, when there's nobody looking at them?

A leg cramp seized him, in the long water-muscles he'd kept to training-pitch in all the canals of the Low Countries, and the lochs of Britain too. He got up from the floor, hobbling it out. Emplaning did it every time—hours with his knees locked like a jumping jack's. He was too tall ever to be a top swimmer anyway. Schlomping bonily down the hall to the commissary he'd spotted last night, he flipped a quart of milk into himself from the one of the fridges, feeling very American for still liking milk, then ducked into a Women's, the only can he could find, and padded back. One flaw here—no pool. If that was the real flaw.

The wall lured like a lotus-pond.

Ten years back, in a boarding school—one, like his swimming, of second rank—he and Betts, both from homes where people were silent except when in company, had vowed each to talk aloud to himself when alone, as a form of mind-expansion. His friend reporting success in it, but he never. Contrarily he admired the swimming team's best, a Norfolk boy who got through the extracurricular world on the one word. "Hahyadoin'?" In the mornin' and the evenin'.

Night before last, in London, he had caught an old samurai flick, locally dubbed, Elizabethan-style.

Hahyadoin', Bronstein . . . Well-met! How now?

He touched the wall, piano delicate. One shouldn't have to touch.

Eagle Eye

Suddenly—he was standing close—he stretched himself against the glum metal, arms wide. Laid his head on it.

How—in what way—could you ask the computer to give you back your life? If properly fed, it could put into motion—what you already were. It could give back only the impulses one gave it—as if God could become a mechanical bore, with a Horatio Alger countenance that wouldn't necessarily shine, but harbored information like a grudge. Wasn't a god of course, anymore than your own brain was—which it fearfully resembled. But if one day you fed it all the clues of meditation that you had with you, the little blurts and jargons that kept you going but hidden, and meant you to yourself like your own vibration in the dark—what could happen? What would come back to you? A bad poem to which you could claim authorship? A mumbo-jumbo music in which anybody could hear his own multiples, according to his own programming? Indian warcries, made by American boys on an Italian lake. Or the whooping-cough summer when you ranged back and forth like a monkey put out to sun, the smallest dictator in the world, staring down on the people below, the gray west wall of Central Park, and the viaduct entrance that cut east from the Elba of his own fire-escape.

That kid, himself in the first habitat he knew, had later on taken a primary course in computers in the tenth grade. No mystery, except of knowing. No rocks changed into feathers, except in the nature of things.

About the same ethic too; you could confuddle the other boys or out-equate them, but ended up cheated—as in the best bibles—if you cheated on yourself. It had been one of the phases of his boyhood that he had passed through, tired of and yet kept a romance of—as if he had once owned a bike with a seventh speed on it that went to Samarkand, or had trained on a punching-bag that talked back.

This set-up belonged to his father. The family computer, though he had never seen it before—why shouldn't it serve him in the person as the other household machines would have: washing his shorts, microwaving a steak for his gut, or massaging the inch of maturity that must have fattened on him since last night? Or like all the new maids of the last few years, who had started up like robots when he walked in on them.

It looked like as good a home as any. Jazzy light on the facade and inside, a hoard of secrets you would expect to pay for, in exchange for entering the only orifice where you felt temporarily permanent. Like a cross between a woman and a bank, and inspiring about the same clichés. When he'd been living in it long enough, it might tell him whether he ought to have called up a girl called Jasmin, or should wait for the stewardess due in on Friday next.

When all he wanted was for it to take him by the hand like an infallible nurse, and lead him to where his future was indissoluble from his past, friends passing and repassing in a guild he knew. As much ask that geode on the desk there to float in the downtown harbor—which now that he looked, was checkered with the astral light of all the money around here that was so different from dollarbills.

Hit it—maybe it would give him a dime.

He squatted on his heels. Stayed there sweating, until he heard something. Bald sighs, absent bumpings, from a long way back. Shannon the doorman's all-day minstrel shuffle, their twin orange heads meeting in the elevator shill-game. Dropped me a coin, boyo, can you find it? Found it—your young eyes are sharp. Crafty pink face above his own, as Shannon palmed it. On bad days the quarter became a penny—thief are you; on good days the penny became a dime. And a pat-on-the-back, Eagle Eye, for being half-Irish.

He hadn't had to touch the wall, really.

"How now?" he said.

There was a terrible fragility about the Bronsteins. That they didn't know of. Their kid did his best to act accordingly. In all the Boy's Lives of famous men he had ever read, there was this simple beginning, in which the boy was held transparent in the vial of family, to grow. While the life put one foot after another, scattering little grenades of bread that even in the city would one day lead out of the forest, in single file.

They all three thought they were leading a linear life.

Until Bronstein was eleven, he and his mother and

father had been living "almost forever"—five years—in what his mother also described to whomever hadn't been there yet, as "a nice old-fashioned apartment-house, one of the oldies off Madison." Many such people did get there, to one of the Bronstein cocktail parties—-snagged by his mother at the PTA or even the supermarket, and once on a Saturday afternoon in the aisles of Charles & Co., over a basket of what his mother called "Gormay."

Whenever Maeve felt sad over her age (which was thirty-six in her conversation and two years more on her driver's license), or because the three of them were without a family circle in the neighborhood, or perhaps if a broken promise from a tailor or a maid had left her standing in the kitchen—"high-heeled and pretty as a rose" as old Shannon had once said to her—but realizing once again how alone one could be here—she went shopping. Whirling on the hat, shoes and bag she had bought last time—one had to impress the salesclerks—she would leave in a rush for some cooked-up something she had to have.

Until a few years back, Bunty had been part of it, either on those short forays—when she returned, larky and undisappointed, to tell his father "there was nothing in the stores, nothing"—or those long days when she and he left "before they open" to get his school-clothes, and ended up in the salons, the housefurnishings, the modern-design corners, the bathshops, the accessories—in any part of the huge, growing storehouse

15

of his mother's alarming but fascinating needs. Nowadays when she left like that, casting back at him mournfully, "Ah Bunty, we used to have nice times then, didn't we?" he saw the dead image of those two, plodding down the aisles. Whole hunks of his childhood had been spent tagging at her hot, absent hand, peeing in ladies' washrooms, sitting tall at table between packages his mother counted and fondled, while she ordered his creamcheese-and-nut. He already understood though, that a purchase was the *most,* and innately serious. His first erotic feeling was that he had been born of such a time, in just such a conjunction.

"Imaginary errands, Maeve, you live on them," his father said. Indeed her closets were full of them. If so, could they still be considered imaginary? Bunty decided against asking. He already knew he was expected to get his brains from his father, and his looks from her. Both seemed satisfied with the arrangement. He was still uneasy with it.

"Maeve MacNeil, secretary, married Buddy Bronstein, her boss," his father would say, twinkling. "An old New York story."

"He means 'Abie's Irish Rose'," she answered, smiling. Both of them explained this to him with zest.

"But you're both *white,*" Bunty said.

Sometime after this, they moved east to the Madison Avenue place.

He liked them both okay. Loved them apparently, as when the doctor they had begun to call their "family"

one, after explaining sex to him, which Bunty kindly
tolerated, looked up sharp over his really too-much black
rims, and said, "Love your folks, Bunty lad?", and he
had answered surprised, "Why not?" Pressed, he had
said "Sure," and was released. Telling the last of his
West Side cronies—Ike Israelson, who in homework visits clearly had folks who suffered from too much
neighborhood family—Ike had said, wisenheimer, "He
only wanted to know whether you'd had it yet." Neither
he nor Ike had. "Aren't they something?", Ike said. The
Bronsteins had a new doctor now, on the East Side.

He still couldn't believe, though, that all these successive people could disappear out of a life. Because
that was connected with the possibility of people, being
lost altogether, to themselves as well. The world rested,
an up-side down pyramid, on himself, a reverse Atlas,
at the small end. He couldn't disappear, because the
world would go with him. A fraction. But he in turn
was diminished, as those he knew—small daily corner-
stones—went away from him. Didn't he vanish, crumb
by crumb of him, as they were sucked into the unoccupied
space around us, which is wherever we are not? And
ultimately this connected with the disappearance of all
the people who ever had been, who were presumed
to be waiting for resurrection somewhere. He didn't
really believe that either; when you thought of the
numbers, of the amount of earth it would take to hold
them,—was there enough even if one took in the Tibetan
mountains, the Serengeti, the world of ice above Alaska,

17

the Faroe islands—all that? He went to the American Museum of Natural History, studied the fossil stones, and saw how unnatural it would be to expect any-thing—as if souls were like eggs, to be storaged some-where.

Yet he kept firm in his trust that all those he knew, or had known or would ever know, would always have a place, someplace. So since each person must be his kind of pyramid—he admitted that—maybe everybody, all told and down the ages, did have a place somewhere.

Ike, whose grandfather had served in the Abraham Lincoln Brigade and lived to tell of it, had been going to be a military historian. Only way, Ike had said, to deal with war. He'd expect to be exempted in order to chronicle it, he'd said shrewdly. Around a corner he used to come yelling—"Trapped on the Meuse! Remember Verdun!"—he preferred wars that were way back. Once in a while, even long after the Bronsteins moved to off Madison, Bunty, yearning a little, could remember his face. Slowly he'd begun to build up a confidence that one day he would run into Ike again, that some day, in the New York way, he would run into them all.

Maeve and Quentin—Buddy, like Bunty, was a nick-name—generally lived with him in the state of equidistance all three felt was normal, and safe. His own reality was like a bubble's in a pot, always breaking into new bubbles, on the liquid effusion of sunsets and stomach-aches in which he sank at night and next morning rose, with all his small wits. He came to know that now and then there was more; they could get to him. Their respective sadnesses interested him: how his mother's was sometimes a woman's sadness; his father's a man's. How this sadness was sometimes private, sometimes mutual and joined.

Usually he stood apart from them at these times because he didn't have it. At first he seemed to himself lower than them, because of his lack (by this time he took for granted that everybody was trying to find a merit that would justify them for being). Gradually he took himself to be higher, or at least out of the circumstances. This happened whenever his parents' conjoining mood, flowering like an embrace, hovered over "what it took to live here." Not only money; though that of course came into it; where you lived and how, came in as much. With who and what people were around. This last, rarely said, he would often hear, like the tinny overtones on his father's old Kranich & Bach piano, inherited from *his* boyhood, and the one piece of furniture they always took along with them.

What he could never hear fully was what they were yearning for, comfortable as they all were, and getting more so. Everything they wanted seemed to be flowing toward them. In his father's office, ever larger on each state visit, lines of desks were starred with faces Bunty didn't know anymore, or who didn't know him. At home, sofas overflowing with pillows, the beds changed for posture ones, and pictures of a kind he had never seen before on his home walls. What was this yearning that went always a little ahead? Now they had it, now they didn't; they had some of it, would they get all of it?—their faces said to him as they stood there. Maeve the redhead, with her narrow bones, fine skin and freckled hands whose large joints she complained of, was three inches taller. To Bunt, already taller than both, his father now looked endearingly small and solid, his face cherub-nice, not cherub-nasty—a teacher had taught him the difference. "The nicest smart man I ever met," one of the desks had confided. "Is he ever gonna get places. You watch."

Where? Though he was involved and grew to know when he was, he wasn't the main focus of it or of them; he could stay subterranean. Or—when he felt it did momentarily light on him, like over a school or a Sunday suit—scornfully above. Even though he hadn't yet identified the nature of this pot of gold that kept them dancing—except that it wasn't just gold. Probably it was like sex, he decided, staring at them with eyes that were conceded to be Buddy's, twitching the ears on a head only just darker red than hers, pursing a wider version of her mouth, and squinting through specs with the same correction Buddy had had at his age, and outgrown. And possibly, like sex, once you had it, as Ike had said, you'd always want it. The thing traveled ahead. Zitkower, his present crony, was a Polish-Hungarian Catholic, and couldn't be asked.

"Boy, can you pick 'em," the maid said when he

20

brought Zitkower home, the last of five Bunt had been carefully trying out in succession since he'd switched schools, and the craziest looking. The maid, already onto the standards of the Bronstein house, stuffed them all to the gills with goodies anyway, and Bunt ignored the comment; he knew certain flaws in her she wasn't aware of—like those pointy nails and the white-cracker way she had with the cigs—and which only he knew had to do with what propelled the Bronsteins, would soon make them give her notice, before he had to go through the pain of finding she had a name and a character he might learn to cherish. His final allegiance had been to a colored girl anyway, Marlene. Real Southern, not Haitian. The last of whom he had been scared of and had caused to vanish, he rather thought, by squinting eagle-eye and mentioning the *Tontons Macoutes*. After that, the Bronsteins had begun shakily ascending the ladder of another kind of help altogether, called by the agency "ethnic American," and so far, no improvement.

He was pretty satisfied with Zitkower. Since coming into the new school district, he had had no one. Had to be somebody neither a toady or to be toadied to, brainy but not all bookish, a natural apartment-house kid—some of the ones moving in or back from the suburbs were too much, and not a creep—like the three in his grade who had just shaved themselves tonsures. Just somebody with a little motherwit, and on roughly the same standing generally. Like Ike.

Witold, shortened to Witty, had also just moved

21

in from Central Park West. Their rooms had been bigger up there, too, and though their present decor was nothing like the Bronsteins', or the maid's either, but crabbedly middle-Europe on both counts, the food for alternate homework visits was good and plentiful, in that style. There was the same sense too of a current flowing through the house upgrade. And about to dislodge it, though at the Zitkower's the brains were differently divided. Witty's father, second-in-command of a restaurant and also a wine authority, was already talking of an apartment with a real dining-room, in a tone Bunt recognized. Obscure, and reaching. And sad.

"You'll get it," Bunt said. Aloud. Surprising himself.

"What are you, a magician?" Mr. Zitkower —"Zit"—said.

"Nah, just an authority on real estate," Witty had been to Bunt's room and knew he always saved over the Sunday section and read the listings with a mixture of anticipation and gloom.

Mrs. Zit, an interpreter for the UN, was the brainy side, though she spoke suddenly from behind her book—and clearly not for the first time, of "moving out." The suburbs.

"I won't go," Witty said. "The kids coming in from there are impossible. And you should *see* the Catholics." He wore a large ivory cross, hung on a wire which induced a rash on his neck but which he wouldn't change, and had just initiated the school to the skinhead style of hair. The cross was a put-on; he was a regressed choir-boy. Not at all bookish, but the Jesuits had given him a good, firm way with the studying. And he was an only. An only child. Bunt's tries with those who weren't had never been quite as comfortable. And one with the daring—Bunt's mouth had fallen open—to say what he just had. Though the Bronsteins never poached socially on the families of boys he brought home, and Bunt was grateful for it, he now wondered if he mightn't introduce to them the Zitkowers, perhaps invite them to one of Maeve's "do's" as she was now calling them, or get his parents invited to the Z's Sunday open-house. He saw himself and Witty on the sidelines, picking it all up, Witty's head shifting side to side like a sparrow's and not only from the eczema—and his own eagle-sight. Then, at the appropriate time, they could discuss and define this current that was in their families, this energetic sadness that was so much the same.

At this time, he had about accepted, out of the mouths of his parents, that New York was to blame. These days, a Saturday mood overtook Maeve that both the Quentins—Buddy and Bunt—recognized. This would come on after the football scores, or mid-way through the opera, before evening, and always when his parents had no evening date. The weekend shopping had been done, that morning at the latest. But there would still be time to buy something. Or to see the streets. Or to meet somebody they might know. Or to acquire somebody they knew slightly, to know better.

"Look, I feel New Yorky," his mother would cry.

"Let's go to Sherry's before it closes. Or to Charles's. Let's go get some gormay." On the way out she would swing her basket almost vertically. "Watch it, Maeve, you'll crown me," his father would say, but he always went amicably, more recently shooting a look at Bunt which thrilled him. Now and then his father said "I'll go for you, or Bunt will. What's your need?" Running to check her make-up she batted a hand at him.

Say one thing, he remembered those walks, most of them cold ones. Their summers went another way, he to camps, they to trips, in a set-up which did have a kind of boring permanence. On the walks their family connection became clearer, almost stately. Just at that hour they could saunter, wistful but comfy. Triviality swayed in the air, all the nice kinds—smoke rounding from lips, wind in skirts, and block after block a peculiar under-rhythm like a smile stretching and waning, as people toddled to the plateglass, worshipful, and receded warmer than they had been. It was holy to shop. Yet if he ever had his own sadness it might begin on these walks.

Home lingered at the other end of the snail-trail they had left behind them, getting to be a bright, jazzy place with known corners to be knuckled into and settled on, knee-lift chairs for Buddy's business-wracked bones, and the hot dinner left early by the help, for Maeve to queen over in her housecoat of the week. Away from it now, home was boring to remember, with an edge of pain in that—but the kind of place he must be grateful for. To be so, he had only to remind himself of certain school sermons and movies. Usually he bent his head into his chest, closed his eyes wherever he was and said sternly within his mind-cage: *Concentration Camp.* And it was true that the street, buzzing familiarly at all hours under the same mysterious sky, made him want to flail his arms and streak off—to be lonely and somewhere homebent at the same time.

"Beautiful," Buddy said. "Look at it. And that. Maeve, did you see it? Her." A couple had just passed, done up for the evening.

"Did you see him?"

They flirted, to show him they were wedded for life.

"There's that model I was telling you about." They stopped in front of a Jag he would swop any day for a Honda. "Lefthand drive though. But that's the color."

"Bronze . . . I've been thinking of a pair of bronze shoes but I wouldn't know where to. Kid. Custom-made I'd have to, probably."

He swung between their errands, long since able to tell which could or would harden into fact, and which would remain to travel ahead of them.

"What a night it is," his father said tenderly. When Buddy blessed the weather, he felt happy; the weather could be anything. Most people were the other way round, but his father could see an environment, gauge it and maybe get it, before it saw him. "But it's been a week. I'll be glad to stay home."

Eagle Eye

His mother was looking in a shop window full of towels Buddy thought he'd seen somewhere. "Yes, I *bought* some. Italian—aren't they great? But that bathroom gets seamier and seamier. Still, where we are, we have two finally."

"Oh not finally. Not for you, Maeve. And I'm with you. But not this year. The office is moving up. And I may have something there that'll surprise you. Then . . . we might even look for a co-op." He caught Bunt's arm and swung along with him.

A pang went through him, that he might ever want to dwarf the world like them.

He still didn't like his new room; the corners were not the same. Witty's room had stayed the same wherever; he said their whole place, full of ikons, samovars and embroidered stuff, always did, no matter how they enlarged it. Maybe it was because they were Catholic. Maeve was, but it wasn't the same. She and his father had offered him the choice: Be like she'd been, or a Jew like Buddy had. He had no reason to; it was all in the past for them. "But maybe you'd like it," he'd said, thinking of the sadness. "Church." They had crowed at him. He always earned credit for smartness the wrong way.

Now he put his head down and said some words to his ungrateful self.

"What's that you're saying?" his father said as they swung into Charles & Co. "K-k-k- what?"

26

"Nothing." It was his old stutter. *K-k-k.* "C-c-c co-op."

Maeve's basket filled slowly with stuff they would never use except maybe the biscuits; she always bought one of anything she didn't know.

"Calamari," Buddy said. "We'll never use it. That's squid."

"When I was a kid on the farm, my mother bought artichokes because we couldn't grow them, and made us eat them. So when we grew up, we'd know how."

"Why she won't come down—" Buddy said. "She could have them every night."

And Maeve said as usual "It's not the artichokes."

They had gone through all this before. Groceries seemed to bring it out in her. When Maeve's father died, they had finally visited the farm in Amenia, New York. A stark white house, and the great swelling road, blond-green with spring then, rising to where the Berkshires cracked wide.

"God, what a generous countryside that was."

Buddy meant that the people were meancolored, which he and Bunty had confided to each other—gray and blue tints to their skins, as if they'd never been farmers at all. Diet, his father said, but it was plain that he too was depressed by what he saw. Mr. MacNeil, the grandfather never yet seen, was a peanuty corpse with a floss of white on top, and a mick mouth which Maeve's and his own were said to resemble. They were not like any Irish Buddy had even seen—no drinks, for one thing. Bunty, on whom great hope had been placed—"Be sure to say Granma MacNeil"—had not been a success—even his red hair and Maeve's was a throwback, Mrs. MacNeil said, none of theirs.

This did fascinate him. "Don't you own your own throwbacks?"

She had a triangular jaw like a cat's, a heart probably of cat-size also, and a set of thin coin-silver spoons, much valued, and often described by his mother. He had tried to steal a spoon for her. "What are you doing, Jew-brat?" After the visit, the three of them had driven straight north, through the blue gap in the mountains, to a Treadway Inn where they stopped for the night, and he saw his parents drunk for the only time. They were drunk at each other. "Don't you dare send her money, Buddy," Maeve had said. "To have it thrown back to you. That I'm living like she wanted me to, with *you*. Don't you ever dare."

Sometimes he had a fantasy of summer there, the blackberry brambles fruited now, and the warm, consoling flanks of cows.

"You could send her the calamari," he said now. "Your whole gormay shelf." Which Maeve catalogued carefully, studying the labels, then left.

Maeve choked. Buddy's face, never too small for affection, smiled lopsided. Like the cow, against whose side Bunty had put his own shamed head, he had consoled.

28

Though Buddy's parents were dead, and a successful brother and sister lived in California—visits mutually planned but never yet made—he still scattered money constantly through remnant Brooklyn counsins, and was always invited to all weddings and bar mitzvahs, buying Bunty a yarmulka for the first of those, and touting the warm family life they would find there. Now and then a cousin dropped by apologetically; Manhattan did not appeal to them. " 'With a store like A&S,' " Buddy quoted, " 'who needs a Korvette's? Waddya need all the push?' They must be the last hold-outs in Flatbush. And now maybe they have the Korvette's."

In Charles's that afternoon, a woman standing near smiled at Maeve. "Scrimshaw. Your bag." She had short white hair, blue-chip eyes, and a tweedy air of well-being. "Nantucket?"

Maeve nodded down at the small straw bag with the bone plaque on its lid, scratched with a picture of a whale. Easter before last, when they had been up there for a couple of weeks, Maeve had spied certain women carrying them like badges—permanent residents, she said, not tourists like them. When the shop-owner, pleading a long waiting list, had refused them, Buddy had ferreted out the carver, who had some old work—not for sale. There had been correspondence. The carver's name became a household one. "Eighteen months and three hundred smackers," Buddy had said, opening the package. "But here you are, Maeve, here's your fishingcreel."

29

"I have one, of course, but nothing so fine ... Wherever? ... Excuse me, I'm Elinor Reeves, we live in the old Berry house ... Don't think we've met up there."

"No, we haven't been for some years," Maeve said. "We go to Italy now."

They had gone to an Italian spa for Buddy's relaxation—"Wuddya know, I have a liver now," his father said joking—for three weeks last spring.

"I wanted to order one for mother. Hers fell overboard. Our sloop. But the ones the shop gets are nothing like hers was. Or like this."

"If you know the carver," Maeve said. "Sometimes he'll do a little better for you. I'm afraid I can't think of the name just now. But I have it at home."

Buddy gave a snuffle, covered by the handkerchief he took without hurry from his breastpocket. He got away with a lot of such hamming, Bunty now observed, because of his gestures being in a small radius.

"Oh, would you? May I call? Or my secretary. I'm just catching a plane."

"I'll phone you, Mrs. Reeves." Maeve had on the mick charm-smile Bunty formally denied himself if he thought of it. "I know who you are."

"Oh ... thank you very much."

"I heard you at the club. Quite a few of our friends are your wellwishers." She introduced Buddy. "Maybe you'd like to join us to meet them some Wednesday afternoon at our home. Maybe a week from next."

"Wednesday . . . now let's see—"

"Any Wednesday," Maeve said. "It's my afternoon."

When the woman left, Buddy said, "Since when?"

"Since now." Maeve giggled.

"*What* club?"

"The precinct one. A girl I met at the PTA goes to it. I meant to."

"Aha. That Mrs. Reeves. Maeve I have to hand it to you. She'll have to come."

"Why?" Bunty said.

"She's running for Assembly," his father said. "But why Wednesday?"

"They have a house in Delaware. They fly down every weekend, I hear. In a private plane. She often stops in here before."

"Why, *Maeve*."

"Then they must use the stuff she buys," he said.

"Shut up, Bunt," his father said. On the way out, he added "I won't be sore though, giving up those Sundays. Looking forward to enjoying my posture chair."

"Not giving them up." Maeve pushed forward into the wind like a masthead.

Buddy groaned. "That ragtail and bobtail."

"It'll get better. You'll see."

"Cocktails. When Bunty and I are practically the only males."

"Bring some from the office."

These days, at any mention of the office, where his mother never went now even with him, his father turned vague. "Changes are being made. Maybe later on, Maeve. Not just now." He turned full at her though, so she could see his smile. "Anyhow, you sure learn quick."

"People have to go somewhere on Sunday. Even *wanted* people. I came from a small town. I know."

"Maeve . . ." Buddy said. "Want to go to a show tonight? I've got an in with that ticket broker at the Waldorf. We could."

When his mother's face broke open like that he could see why Witty had called her a sparkle-plenty dame, and had approved her legs. She shifted her head then, slightly toward himself.

"Bunty, you're old enough to stay alone," his father said. "Aren't you?"

"Sure." He straightened up and made his heels ring. We can't embarrass him much longer with a sitter, Buddy had said to her in the bathroom sometime back. The two bathrooms, his and theirs, were end to end, and the old building not as soundproof as Maeve made out; what he heard there would have been useful found goods, except that the Bunty discussed there seemed not himself but a kind of mule-stupid dollbaby he scarcely recognized.

"Maybe I'll call Witkower." He would never. He would hanker to, but never trust himself near the phone, to cross the weekend barrier. Four times a night, some schooldays, but tonight, what Witty would think? Foreigners—they probably had a huge family intimacy going.

Home came quickly. The street was never that mysterious, going back. He stood in the foyer his mother had set up with a mirror, chest and chair, though not the same ones, and tried to remember the last foyer. He already knew what it was like to be alone here—they'd forgotten they had already left him, once. Now and then it was a little scary, if you had one of those moments when you looked at your hands, saw your feet, shifted awareness with a jolt, realizing for an eerie minute that you were—yourself. And the place was not consoling.

Maeve was marking the calendar by the phone. "Wednesday," she muttered.

Buddy smiled at him. "Your mother's the smartest little secretary a man ever had." He seemed dimmer, Quentin again.

"I'm not sure I don't think Witty is too old for you," Maeve said, turning suddenly. He had a feeling she might grab him, the bathroom Bunty, and whip him off to a department store. She was always Maeve. Buddy was Quentin also; he would never make Bunt his pawn. He had said Bunt was old enough. Funny though, how they never saw the real things were where you had to have your alternatives. It was possible to think them shabby. But he would never be ashamed of them.

"That Mrs. Reeves," he said. "Her mother must be a million years old."

He could always break them up. That cheered him.

Already he had begun to feel himself the guardian of the real things—though he didn't yet know what these were.

Eagle Eye

◻

Mrs. Reeves was unable after all to come to them on the Wednesday arranged for her—on what he heard the gathered women tell one another was a perfectly good excuse. But one Sunday weeks later, met by the Bronsteins, who were laden with last-minute cocktail items, she had surprisingly come back with them. It was a dark day, perhaps no planes were flying, her unsuccessful campaign was over, and as Bunty was helping fix the hors d'oeuvre, he heard his parents say there were rumors her husband had asked for a divorce. Certainly she had appeared alternately gay and distracted in a halting way, and wanting to be near any transient warmth, even theirs—as if she might be having one of those moments when she knew she was herself. In the intervening weeks he himself had grown used to these; his parents went out many weekend nights now, and he never called Wit.

As their lone guest at first, Mrs. Reeves had been calmed by their devoted cocktail attentions, later greeting civilly each of the "the week's pickups," as Buddy called them—the man from the Arthur Murray dance studio—in whose group Maeve had once been, the Bronsteins' dentist's assistant and her new fiancé, also one of Bunt's teachers and the reedy vocal coach who lived with his spaniel-faced friend on the ground-floor.

34

"Oh yes," Bunt heard Buddy say later that night, on the other side of the bathroom wall. "She treated us all with the consideration of a candidate."

"Buddy—" Maeve said. "She lost."

"It was the house that got all her impertinence, Maeve—didn't you see?"

Reeves'd been angry for sure to find herself here, and went for the house instead of them. "Boy—" she'd said to him as he passed her the first plate of his own hors d'oeuvre—(out of boredom, and some interest in the company, any company on the long Sunday, he'd become adept at getting tins open and their contents into praisedly weird combos)—"boy, what is that awful thing over there—a girandole?"

He knew she shouldn't speak that way to him, and stared at her until she dropped her eyes and asked him, in her Nantucket voice, where he was at school. "Ah yes, that's the one people move in for." But she seemed to calm herself again, now that he had made her realize he was a child, and asked him if he played that nice old upright piano.

"No, my father used to. It's the only thing here that's really ours." Which since all this lot had been acquired at Bloomingdale's, was what he felt. He'd made her one more polite offer of his tray, pretending meanwhile that he was at diplomatic reception—at school his class was doing careers and he had chosen as his project Ambassador—and had moved on. He'd just been considering whether the tray wasn't a flaw in his role, when the coach and his friend came up. "How'd you get the name Bunty?" they said in chorus. Rehearsed it maybe, the way Buddy could sometimes be heard in low-voiced shaving monologue, speaking to the trade. Did his mother's guests all look so uneasy because they were here, or because they were themselves?

"It's a Little League connosh . . . connotiation," Bunt said, in character, then ambled into the kitchen, where he dumped tray and responsibility, walked on down the hall as a third secretary of the legation, and landed on his bed, kicking up his heels in a high mystic glee which had to be shared. His wealth of gathering experience dazzled him, but at the same time he had to confirm the world with his own kind, even if all he said when Witty came to the phone was "How's tricks?" Lately, though they were still close, Witkower had taken to girls, advising "Get onto it, Bronstein," and Bunty, since his thirteenth birthday, had taken one to the Modern several times. Tonight, Wit had said "Jesus, what a weekend!" the minute he picked up, giving Bunt scarcely time to recall the barrier which had been crossed. "Jesus, am I glad you called."

They were deep in Wit's story when his parents, showing Mrs. Reeves the house, had knocked at his open door. "Hold it Wit—" he'd said. "Here's folks."

With what had happened to Witkower, this bathroom corner to which he'd retreated once the party was over, was likely to be his closest crony for sometime. It had a chair whose marine-blue fur—matched to the Anchors Aweigh bedroom pattern his father called

"Macy's-by-the-sea"—had worn off comfortably under his bottom, and the paint above the tiles was solid with the pinups of a lifetime; he even studied here. Until now he'd also valued it for the voices on the other side of the wall. Though he felt guilty when they talked about him, the natural opacity of parents was such that without this extra he would never have understood them. Tonight, hearing them really fight for the first time, even then raising issues more than voices, he caught onto why they spent so much time together in there. Though they must have heard him wash and flush his toilet when he remembered to, since he had no one to talk with it was the one place in the house where they felt soundproof from him.

"Yes, the house got it. But it won't always, Buddy. You'll see."

He knew that voice, excited with its own despair. Nothing in the stores, for tonight.

"You'll see. By next year."

"Not next year, Maeve."

"You moved the office," his mother said.

He began to study a break in the tiles near his right foot. With his left eye closed, it looked like a lion's head. With his right, the rhomboid pattern itself pushed forward. With both eyes open, it was only a floor. Pretty soon he could expect to forget Wit's face. The features, that is. Now and then—as had happened for a while with Ike, who was now only a name and a feeling—he could also expect the whole face to flash back.

"Moved the—is that all it means to you? I changed

my whole—life. Papa, he would've done handsprings all the way from Maiden Lane to the docks. And you don't even come downtown to see."

"Because I'm your wife, not your father. Where I live is here."

"Where you live—" Quentin said. "Who knows? When you can let that woman say that to you. And let it pass."

Entering his room talking, Mrs. Reeves had posed there, once again herself as when she had first met them. He'd hung up the phone, whispering Wit a quick goodbye. Maybe they'd see each other again, probably not.

"Good grief," Mrs. Reeves had said, surveying his blue cork bunk with the hawsered bedspread—real rope—and himself, miserably back of the foc'sle wheel where the phone was. "Good grief, what do people imagine children *think*!"

He hadn't ever considered. What people could think, had thought about Witkower, was what interested him. What they thought about everything.

"Your wife says you're looking for a co-op, Mr. Bronstein. If you're new here, you'll find some of the older ones further over our way have a nice country feeling."

What children could see was that she'd had a drink or two.

Fingering her pearls, she held them draped at her shoulder. "I must say, these furnished flats are the very worst."

He'd looked up then, at Maeve. Buddy was watching her. Neither had laughed, as expected.

No sweat. "Nobody pays us to laugh," Witty had hummed at their last movie together—the same song he was always on. Witkower had been caught on a sofa with a girl, and was being transferred to a Catholic school. A preppy one, out-of-town. What his folks took most serious, Witty had said, was that when they'd gone on about making the girl pregnant, he'd told them he'd used something. "Well, nobody pays us to laugh," Wit said on the phone. " 'No-ho-body pays us to cry-y.' "

What Bunt wanted to ask, he couldn't—had Wit been wearing his ivory cross at the time, or hadn't he? But neither Witty nor he would ever call back anyway. Wit had joined the lost ones who never wailed but were an increasing, silent panel in the back of his mind. They never wailed because they didn't know they were lost.

"Why did you lie to her Maeve? In front of your own son."

"I didn't lie."

"You didn't deny."

"In front of you, you mean. You're just sore because she thought you were new. When your father came here in nineteen-oh five."

Buddy gave a laugh. "Everybody's always new in New York. But maybe you have to be born here to know."

After a pause, Buddy said "You won't come downtown? You could have a lot of range these days. Partners even. In a way."

"Ah Buddy. Hon, listen. I know you mean well.

39

And I know you don't mean it for real—don't I know how you operate? No. Listen. There's a kind of girl lives around here. Within about twenty blocks. Not the younger ones. The young married ones. Cool . . . you can spot them anywhere. Not always the society ones. Not dumb. Busy, too. But their position in life is very clear. Their men make the waves downtown. They float along with them . . . I want to be one of those. Ten years on."

"You wanted to be, Maeve. At our age, nobody floats."

He'd grown sleepy and had pulled out his math homework. He was good at it; Buddy had helped him to be. Math was like the dream behind the money, his father said. He'd about finished one set of problems when Maeve said, "Maybe . . . the country, Buddy? Not too far up for you. But where it's friendlier because everybody *is* new. And I'll get somebody to help me fix up the house. Because I tend to overdo. You know that." The way she spoke, so earnest and down-to-earth, she must have cried. "You'll be proud of it. You can bring people up for weekends. You're better at that too. Not from the office maybe. But from New York."

He waited for Bud's answer.

"I don't know, Maeve. Horses? Golf? You have to have an interest anywhere you are. Make connections. Or it can be deadly there too."

"Not Westchester. Maybe the Sound. A Nantuckety little house." She giggled.

"And you have just the handbag for it. No, not this year. After that, I'm with you. But not yet."

"You might even commute to lower Manhattan by boat. I've heard of that."

"Couple of my—new associates—do it," Quentin said. "It *is* healthy."

Bunty sat up. His father loved water, the bigness he said it gave to a house, or a man. Or to a family in view of it. Or to a city. Back in Amenia he had talked of it. "Funny," he'd said to Bunty, "how mountains can make for mean minds. No wonder your mother wanted out."

"And for Bunty. Buddy. The teens are bad here."

He let his books slide, half hoping they'd hear. Didn't they know what the teeners up there in places like that were like now? Bored to murder, without the streets, Witty'd said; he knew all kinds of stories from the Catholic network. How one group of kids had regularly vandalized the houses of certain sodality women they'd had a hate on. How the Fathers had turned up a Manson-type black-Mass group just in time, in Garden City—and how the young faith in Fort Lee might as well be in flames. For every pair of parents that moved their ten-year-olds out, Witty'd said, there'd soon be twice as many moving their fifteen-year-olds back. Outside their own school, PS 6, Wit'd pointed out some of these older ones calling for their younger sisters and brothers—jocks and girls in purposely debased clothing —dirty jeans below, on top angoras and custom leather—who all drove clamped to their little cars, as if driving snowmobiles. Why Wit should think a bad scene was more sacriligious when it took place in woods and leaves, he couldn't say—except for the cows, maybe. There was a girl in their own grade who pushed dope, and a boy who stole for it. What Wit had done, his parents should give thanks, it was so clean.

"We could send him off to school," Quentin said. "I've been thinking of it. Not that it isn't the same for them everywhere these days."

"In the right town, we wouldn't have to send him away. With the right school. Oh Buddy, forget the co-op. Let me start to look. Why should just Bunty go away; maybe the city's killing all of us. Oh Buddy . . . Quentin . . . let me look."

Bunty stood up. Rootlets in his chest, just healing, had been torn again. If some doctor had asked "Do you love it here?" he'd be cagey. But the streets were mysterious. The flanks of buildings—his eye sometimes leaned on them. Cronies had been. And were possible. No, no, we won't go.

He began beating on the wall to the rhythm of it. Let them kick their sadness by themselves. Home's their concentration camp. Where they send you away, for their sins. He began bawling. "No, No. Nobody pays me to laugh. Nobody pays me to cry." He couldn't remember the last line until much later. *Why should we be staying folks?—for your bye-and-bye.*

They rushed in—through the wall, it seemed to him.

42

He was inviolate in his own childhood—where they could be heard. They would never hear him.

"Not away from the city, Maeve," Buddy said, holding him in his arms. "Away from us."

On the Monday, a year or so later, when they were to move to the Park Avenue place, he was in the lobby at eight AM, sent to wait for the vans; the substitute day man had fouled up the intercom. Shannon, for some reason, wasn't due until noon. After several vans had come from the various thrift shops and Salvation Army—to whom Maeve was giving everything but their personals, he sat on, waiting to say goodbye to Shannon. During the year, this place had become a co-op too. With bright new oriental rugs, a new super who oiled the walnut paneling, and two-thirds new tenants who breezed into their ownership like pioneers. His father agreed the place had picked up wonderfully, but confided to him that it wouldn't be nearly as good a buy as the one they were going to—not when you came to sell.

Before nine o'clock, at least four boys his own age came down with their dogs. Two gave him an interested look when they came back—if Shannon had been there, introductions would have been made. In any case, all the kids here would be going to his old school probably, and under a different calendar from his. Through "influence" which Buddy had suddently pulled out of a hat, against his own principle of never mixing "downtown" and home, Bunty had been admitted to the Lycée, where he would go until he went away to a school in Massachusetts that was holding a place for him. This had been the bargain offered him for their not moving out. He hadn't understood what had scared them so, but since any choices he would've made had retreated into the past, he acceded silently—which worried them more.

The Lycée was cliquey, though the girls were friendlier. He'd already taken a girl named Paulina Vespasi—whose father *was* an Ambassador, and her sidekick Dolly Something, to the Museum of the City of New York. This had come about because of the only Italian he knew, which he had blurted out in the class in *dictée*, where he was very behind. The endlessly linguistic air of the school miffed him anyway. "Altro che!" he had muttered to himself. "Altro *che!*" and she had turned round delightedly. *"Come?"*

At Montecatini, where the doctor had sent his father again, he had met three boys: Perrin, from Manchester, England, Emilio from Siena, and Frank Massler, from Princeton, New Jersey, USA. As an old hand, he was modestly able to show them all the paths and haunts that were useful to the healthier young. "Oh, any place you been *twice*," he said. But it made an emotion. Hotel life, with its known hours and meeting-places, had

44

quickly made them intimates; then the spa had been enveloped for days in scarves of mist and fizzy rain that sent the four of them into huddles, games, doodling on the hotel piano until they were stopped, conspiracies, a few fool tricks on the concierge that he still chortled over—and close talk. Emilio, son of a *professore* and English speaking, had shared his Vespa with them, as well as deadpan tales of his family life, which appeared to take place around an enormous soup plate, or else in the bed where his parents made babies so noisily they always woke the latest one. "But I forgive them everything, for making me a Sienese." Perrin, a thin, glassy-looking boy, was rude to Bunty and Frank in a dirty way that glinted through his stiff manners, but they left him alone, since he and his mother, who was really ill, were here on a shoestring, and he was so knowing about all the monuments they cooked up trips to. Bunty and Frank—a shy boy, good at math also—were required to be authorities on America. Perrin taught all three how to make brass rubbings; it was Emilio who noticed that Bronstein's were the best. At home, buildings new or old were spoken of either as acquisitions or as enemies in a kind of soft war. Here, he and they took to one another, his eyes glossing past people to return to their stony flanks. Nothing since the cows had so affected him.

On the last dusk over there, after scavenging all day for the puny wood and stealing some, they had made a bonfire near a lake. "A tarn," Perrin said in

his competent voice, "anything smelly as this is a tarn."
He had brought chocolate. Emilio was chef. "The Americans catch the rabbits, but don't know how to skin them."
Everything Emilio said sounded like a proverb. High
up, above the brittly leaves that shone without light-
source from the gloomy cloud-castles piling in on their
spot of fire, a ruined donjon clung to a crag. His chest
stretched with yearning—how could he yearn so to be
where he *was?* Everything was so solid. Perrin, cleaning
up the last of the stew in his famished way, said "Why
don't you two—would you teach us, Emilio and me—one
of your American Indian dances?" They saw with dismay
that he wasn't being dirty. For days, (while his mother
coughed up what Frank, whose father was a doctor,
said must be "the last positive TB sputum in civilized
Europe, and that's a national health service for you!").
Perrin, who had seen all the American movies, had been
deep in the *Leatherstocking Tales.*

Emilio had clapped a hand over his own telltale
mouth. Wrinkling his forehead like a saint's, he had
signaled the two others what they must do. Solemnly,
Frank and Bunty had begun doing it, hop-hop into the
war-dance, bending low into their knees, Ugh! Ugh!
They pranced high with the tomahawk, making the ulla-
ulla whoop, palms batted against lips—"Wah-h-h."
Emilio had joined in, then at last, Perrin. Fallen flat
on their backs in a circle, toes in, they lay for awhile
looking up, without laughing. On the trail down, he
saw that the back of the donjon held a line of wash.

Next morning burst through the clouds. "Bright as a berry," Buddy said leaning out a window, his face chastened and thinner. "What a shame, just when we're leaving," Maeve said, slamming it rhythmically into her packing-hand. But Bunty, on his two feet, slouched inside the narrow doorframe with his feet on one side and his shoulders braced against the other, kept on reading a Wall Street Journal he had filched from their room-neighbor's trashbasket; he had ways of dealing with these things now, and had already left.

In the lobby by now, only older people were taking their dogs out. When the new day-man finally called out, "Waitin' for anythin', kid?", and told, answered, "Shannon won't be in today, called in sick", he rose to his feet and height—almost five eleven now—and dealt. Rise to the feet, avoid all corners at these times, lean forward—pro*ject*! Already, at the Lycée, he was projecting forward to a Cheshire Academy he figured to spend only a year in before going to a larger school he had better try for if he was going to Yale to be an architect. His allegiance was all to schools now; he liked to think of that line-up awaiting him. "Tell Shannon good-bye, . . . and a penny from Eagle Eye." He was about to hand over the coin he had been palming since he got down here, then thought better of it. A ten-dollar goldpiece he had got from his grandfather, on Abe's eightieth birthday and his eighth—perhaps he'd better send it, or stop by. He knew he would never stop by.

Outside, he paused, wondering whether Maeve had

47

unwontedly said "Take a cab, we'll meet you there," because Park Avenue required his arriving in that style, then decided it was only her drama-of-the-day and started walking the seventeen blocks down. Just then another van drew up. Couldn't be for the Bronsteins. It was. "Half a van-load, including a piano," the boss mover said. It was the van for the personals. "Grand or upright," the driver said.

"Upright."

"Better be. We don't move grands."

When they had loaded up, he cadged a ride with them. Weren't supposed to, the boss man said, then relented. Couldn't believe Bunty was only the false sixteen he'd said he was, anyway. "Looks like seventeen, don't he, boys? Here kid, stick this cap on your head, they'll think you're only another Irishman. Can't sit up front though; I could be fired for it."

Back of the van was where he wanted. And since the van was even less than half full, and the last thing in—the piano—was securely strapped and shrouded, they let him keep open the door. Laughing at him. At first he let his legs dangle, but that mightn't be too good for their insurance either, so he stood up. Turning a corner in the midst of car-owners sitting lone in their small housings, jogging handsomely over east, then south, over rubble and through the deference of cab-drivers and even busses, he saw the streets as he never had before. Inside the van, there were curved struts, not a straight, dull vanside; the opening where he bal-

anced was shirred like a great horseshoe, canvassed like
an old canteen. Between him and the pile of khaki wrap-
cloths there was really a line of calico curtain. Behind
the calico, somebody lay sick; there was always somebody
sick, in a covered wagon. His eyes were sharp but he
didn't know for what. Not for Indians.

When they rolled up to the awning, the new building, which he hadn't seen yet, turned out to be more
or less like the one he'd left, only bigger. There were
some ornaments though, to distinguish it by. And a new
doorman. He jumped off the truck and watched the
crew of two unload, knowing better than to offer help.
When they came down for the last time, and clapped
the van door closed, he went around front to the cab
with its contents, and held up the cap. "Thanks very
much for the ride. It was super. And please, could I
give you this?"

They were shocked to the gills, he could see that,
and refused at first, meaning it. But he stood his ground.
"Please. The guy it was for back there, didn't show up.
And I'll remember the ride."

"Damtootin' you will." They took the gold coin, vow-
ing to split it between them, or toss for who would keep
it for his kids. Once they'd decided to take it, he saw
he was out of it. When they drove off, he didn't need
to wonder what they said of him. But the ride really
had been of use to him. Like a perspective pointed back,
it had shown him that even if he were to send the goldpiece as planned, carefully wrapped, stamped and

addressed to Doorman, Shannon—a talkative man with all the boys and girls in the house, as well as a man of few phrases—mightn't know who had sent it. Even if Bunt put a return name on it, Shannon mightn't know from which of his brood of eaglets the "penny" had come.

Yes, the new building was made of the same sturdy, dank stone, a solidified gloom that entered the chest, surrounded him from behind, and took him two or three flights up in the elevator to forget. But the apartment, eight rooms, spiked around an anteroom with a weak, white mantel which hung there like a mouth waiting to be shut or stuffed, did have the look of a family place, even in spite of the one feature that gave Maeve such glee. A black-and-white terazzo floor, put in by the last tenant, began at the halldoor like a mad dream of Italy, and stopped well in the field of vision one and a half rooms down.

"What's so funny?" Maeve scowled, under the headscarf she kept for moving-days.

He leaned there hysterically pointing to where the dream floor stopped. "He woke up."

By nightfall the furniture was in and placed; Maeve and a decorator had planned it like a battle this time; they were into Swedish maids now, and a Helga was there to help. His books were in his room. When he complained, with a venom new to him, that one of them—"the one book I needed"—was lost, it was found for him. Whatever his mother was learning, she was very apologetic toward him. In return, he allowed nothing in his room except the servants' bed and dresser that the maid Marlene had once had, a load of bricks he made bookshelves from, and the last tenant's wall-paper, loud as bagpipes, which, as the rest of the place came to a discreet, fawn-gray completion, went off with a bang every time he opened his door. "But your room's so central!" Maeve wailed. No dice; he wouldn't let her change it. Usefully maybe, it taught him the architectural liabilities of a circular house. And brought him and Buddy into what one of the Brooklyn cousins—this time the move had smoked out a few well-wishers snoopy enough to pay Manhattan parking-rates—had called "a lovely relationship between a father and his boy." Buddy often came into his room now to watch TV, dragging his posture-chair.

"What do you think of the joint?" he said one night, swinging the chair to look out at it.

Bunty shrugged. "It looks like—you know—." He shrugged again. Not a joint.

"You could copulate in this place at a teaparty," Buddy said. "The mirrors would be too well-bred to notice it. With twelve Mrs. Reeves's you could do it, God forbid. *And* her mother." Then they went back to TV.

Otherwise, they were all three on even keel again. This place was soundproof for real, and he was glad of it, as the only way to build secrets and wrench his personality away from the Bunty-doll they had bought for him. As Buddy's propositions for him became more acute, he realized that this might always have been the case, but there were hazards there too. The more space his father delicately strained to leave around him for his own growth, the more he thought he could see how his father's space must already be crisscrossed and hedged.

Meanwhile, away at school, where they were being taught to log computers, he and a boy named Betts often went back after hours; cronies sharing only this, like a couple of garage mechanics. The school's two pieces of equipment—one gift horse, one boughten—which were set up in an angle off the science lab that had once been a butler's pantry, and were always breaking down, began to seem to him like a pair of older brothers who had worn themselves out in the service of the young. For a while, no matter what permutations and combinations he practiced, he seemed to be working out some likely simpler tensions in himself. Until a time came when it occurred to him that the more vocabulary he would have, the more complicated would become the offering. The spring day outside the lab window suddenly seemed to him *more*—whatever. And switching to soccer and swimming, he never went back.

One vacation home, coming in from a very adequate day—morning at the Metropolitan Museum, lunch in the Modern's garden, and a two o'clock track meet at the Garden, he found Maeve displaying his room with a certain pride, like the cage of some freak she fondly kept there. He passed her with a swat "Hi, Ma," and went in. Calling her that kept the distance, though "Pa-ing" Buddy was still impossible. Outside ,his closed door he heard the cousin say, "What a nice normal boy!"—Brooklyn's tribute to his short hair, which when longer kept his fair scalp too itchy with pool chlorine. He smiled, his heart pounding as if in fact he'd just made it back to his lair. He knew he was as normal as a boy dared to be these days. He got merely good grades in a class where half were rated as gifted, had just made it up from second swimming team to substitute on first, and was in steady pursuit of three girls, one of whom had already been caught.

EOF—as Betts used to say. END OF FILE

This was the end of the linear life.

▣

The week before he was twenty-one, Quentin wired him to one of his maildrops, the last one. He'd been on a Scottish walking-trip now over—two tents, three men, four girls. "You can come home now from finishing-school," the wire said. He stopped off at the PO in Malleig, apologizing for his dripping boots and hands as if the weather were his, not theirs, and sent a return cable: "Buy a yarmulka for August fifth." The post-mistress, a young woman, wrote it out for him. As he started to spell "yarmulka" aloud, she pushed the slip back at him, accurately done, and he reminded himself that the Scots were the best-educated plain people in the Isles, especially on religion—one more pennyworth of acquired knowledge he would now have to carry home with him. He grinned at her, tipping the soaking tam he had discarded a tarboosh for some weeks back. The twenty-pocketed jacket he wore signaled to any gamekeeper that he was one of earth's exalted, but he had forgotten this. The girl behind the counter was about his age, a buxom bit with the rosy, open face that was always lucky for him, but there was a child by the grate, and as the girl went toward it he saw she had another bun in the oven. On impulse he handed her his father's cable to read. "He means—we've ended the war."

Her hand went to her breast, her mouth quivered for him. "Are you on the run, then? You've been?"

What a sweetheart. In fancy his flesh emigrated back again from the America it was going to, and clove with hers, which would be grooved with all the firm feelings it must harbor: one man, one gun, one cot, one sod.

"N-not officially." He saw his boots had stopped puddling.

They shook hands anyway. As he left, her glance, straying from child to him, was the same for them both.

He knew what it was as well as she; he was a man
—deferred.

Luckier than some. He knew how that went, too.
Buddy's cable made him sore, though—as if his father
had the idea he hadn't thought about it.

By the time he'd left home for his lineup of schools,
all the "better" ones had become expert in the art of
obtaining military exemption—in New England they
were partisan. Sharing with the Pentagon, as a master
had said, a taste for the best material. Halfway through
the tenth grade, they'd already pointed out to him that
if he were to veer just slightly off-center of his stated
interest, to a more mathematically involved one, he
might qualify for a national science fellowship—for
reasons that had nothing to do with need. By the time
he got a draft number, he was onto the fact that the
odds in his crapgame with time were nevertheless better,
since his draft board, whatever its stand on "educational"
deferment, had at hand the great body-pool of New
York. So he'd become part of *his* part of his generation,
of the equilibrating young Americans flying the world
on their trapezes, along with their girls. In summers
and other off-times, or even when a boy's number, a
man's, had been pulled—but while there were still maybe
two kinds of delaying action, or one, or maybe
none—they ate up the world in tramp-travel. Not a dodg-
ing yet, just out on the road. In his nine months abroad
he'd been on a bus to India, a dirty barge in France
and a clean one out of Bruges before he had ever stopped

to stare at a major city; his kind knew rat-corners of the world that even the artists hadn't got to yet.

"Waddya mean—we *are* artists," a big Californian had said to him in a hostel in Wales. "At not doing what we want. Or not finding it out." All the big guy had wanted at the start was to go into the land business in Orange County with his father. "Raise kids and a big fat bankroll—and what woulda been wrong with that?" His blond Tarzan jaw worked belligerently on the target that had escaped. He had boondoggled nearly eight years of school—engineering mostly—through a really ace set of grad school ploys, only to discover, now that the simple life he wanted was legal again, he couldn't get himself to go back to it. He spat on the floor, then looked guilty, suffering from manners he had once had. The hostel was full of ruddy-cheeked eighteen-year-olds from the Midlands, and singing French schoolboys even younger. "I know too much. I'm *twenty-six years old.*" He and his pals didn't usually middle-class it in places like this. "But hell—it *is* armistice." Actually, he hadn't been vulnerable to the draft for some time. When he could no longer explain his inertia, and the home money had stopped, he'd joined up with the hippies for a while, selling leather on the Spanish Steps, doing chalk pavement-pics in front of the National Gallery. "I did blueprints of bombers, from aerodynamics class. One of the profs must of had a defense tie-in." A London paper got onto it, and he was stopped. "Some American general must of walked on it." Hell, he couldn't care less about politics. "Know what my ambition was?" he said, his big angel-lips shaping the word. In the flickering gloom of the hostel, he looked like a boy in a dormitory, whispering what the prefects shouldn't hear. "I wanted to be a *young* father."

His friend in the upper bunk, who after identifying himself as a writing student out of Stanford, had then buried his head, now raised it. The three Americans looked at one another. Names weren't the route these days, as against addresses and food-tips along the way, or an exchange of tags. A fall admission to Yale, architecture and life, Bunty had said. For one year.

"Pol-i-tics," the other student said, looking down at the big boy. "Don't you know what you are? You're a veteran, just like the rest of us. Whether you took a CO, or went to Sweden, or took our route. You're a fatality. Who's alive." He fell back, staring at the low roof, on a splinter of which he had hung his woolen drawers. His aquiline nose brushed them, and his crooked black brows. "You fought your war—to keep your legs and arms, or your balls—or your brain maybe—and now you're being—" He sat up again. "What's that word they called it last time?"

They waited. He was twenty-three, he'd told them, and he attributed his deferments not to his academic fellowship, but to the fact that the town he came from knew his father had died as a naval officer.

"Demobbed." He lay back. He wasn't going home to finish his thesis—a novel. "To Paris, why not? That's where all the second-coming Hemingways went last time or stayed on after; we'll be the third." He already had a pouched vein in one cheek, that jumped like a cud. He knew one of those boys from the Korean war—a guy who by now had been reduced to writing travel stuff for the Sunday sections—but such were the risks. "Gonna live with my girl." The vein moved with his smile, too. "She makes wind-sculpture. It sells." Her father, a wealthy French poulterer, was giving them a shed in Meudon. Lending it. He pulled the hanging underwear over his face until only his nostrils showed, puffing white air. The hostel was at the foot of Mt. Snowdon, and the fire had gone down. Sleepers lay mounded down the vaulted hut in everything they had—duffels, car rugs and plastic ponchos, a sombrero marked "Brighton." Summer soldiers. Bunty put a log on. One of the little Frenchies called out approvingly. They had their own wine.

"My book's a bummer," the upper bunk said.

"You were doing what you wanted, though," Tarzan said.

Sometime during the night, Tarzan skipped, without paying up for his share of the cheese and beer.

"You're lucky," the student said to Bunty the next morning. "Getting out now. It's the grad school hanging around that gets you marble-ized." He smiled. Rightside up and uncovered, he looked mellower. "My girl's expression once. Not this girl. Gotta girl?"

"Not at the moment."

They shook hands and parted. "Look us up in

Meudon, you ever get there. You can't miss it. A big yellow shed." How long "ever" might mean he didn't bother to say.

"Do that," Bunty said. "See you around." He wasn't expected to give his American address. Even if he knew it. Maeve had written him the new one, not long back, but nowadays he always wrote to his father's office anyway. One Chase Plaza. You can't miss.

On the plane home, he made time with one of the stewardesses, who gave him her address in Jackson Heights.

"Quite the Don Juan, aren't you?" the man who was his seatmate said. He was working from a portfolio, had a wedding band, and wore a flowery tie. All of a piece.

"Nah," Bunty said. "It just works out." Since that first girl, Paulina, it more or less had, though he'd never counted—a Don Juan deal that repelled him. Next to the guy next to him though, he was probably an ace, their style.

"Really does, huh? How?"

Bunty turned. No, not a put-down. Except from age fifty to twenty-two. He leaned back, sliding the tarboosh down his forehead. "Stewardesses? Just never shoot the breeze with both of them. Start off right away on only one." And play it harder the nearer New York, or other home bases. When they were going back to whatever they weren't into yet. Or were—and were wondering about it.

The guy was closing his portfolio. Oy. Conversation.

59

"You wouldn't believe it, but a friend of mine once got a dose from one of them, from a stewardess. One of ours, too."

"I guess they get very international."

"You a student?"

"No, I'm in m-mufti." The stewardess passed, and he gave her the nod. "I—f-fought in the war."

"But that was the *other* girl," the guy said. "Or wasn't it." He peered after her down the aisle.

It wasn't. "This is the one that's pushing dope."

"You don't mean it. Good God. So you were over there." He sneaked an uneasy glance at the Egyptian tarboosh, which had been acquired en route from India, in the airport at Nice.

Bunty smiled. "That's a very emotional tie you're wearing, sir." In his best Massachusetts accent.

"Countess Mara. Like it?" The stranger spread a little. Then caught his eye. "You kids. You infernal kids." He launched into an account of his own kids, which since they were several, and all on his tail in various ways, lasted until Kennedy.

As they were filing out, the first stewardess smiled at Bunt. She meant it. His seatmate bent modestly aside, to snag his overcoat from the hatch.

"Not to worry," Bunt said in his ear. "She sounds like a nice girl, lives in Queens. And is thinking of running off to be one of the Children of God. Well, goodbye."

"Good Lord, that's a sect, isn't it. Think twice."

"Oh, I'm looking to be serious. So far, it hasn't worked out."

"Keep trying. Look—my name's Carroll Monteith. Ever want a job in a paper company, come see me. Here's my card."

He was really giving it because Bunty, small deal as he was, was carrying away a piece of the guy's life. The Monteith life.

"Thanks. Thanks very much." The card said "President."

"Branch of course. Of the St. Regis Paper Company."

"Oh I went to camp up there." Their three-word slogan had dotted the virgin forest for five hundred miles. In spite of himself, the urge to swap a piece of life was too strong. "Raped a twelve-year-old girl in those woods once. Mentally. Well—Keep Maine Green."

In the airport, he hoisted the bag Buddy had insisted on sending him from the safari place where he had bought Bunty's presents ever since the thirteenth birthday one—a Camping Companion, otherwise a knife with variously notched blades and many pocket-tools on the side, whose total claimed uses were a minimum of thirty-nine. "No bar mitzvah," Buddy said. "But from now on, you're a pioneer." Beginning to count, from corkscrew to thimble, tiny slide rule to measuring cups, nailfile, pliers and compass, his son had wondered whether his success with Paulina showed. The knife had

61

been stolen from him somewhere back, maybe in the government bar in Amsterdam—El Paradiso—where he had spent a lot of time. But he could still tally its uses, even after he'd lost it, though never getting beyond the guaranteed number. Maybe Tarzan had taken it.

He tucked his head in his chest now and said an admonishing string of syllables to himself; though *K-k-k* and the concentration camps had gone, the impulse or tic had kept on—some nonsense-score that his subconscious kept. Now and then one of these phrases endured long enough for him to link its language with himself more definitely, as people did their dreams. He thought the habit might come from his Catholic heritage, confessive to the end—though it might just as well be a kind of Jewish "touch wood." Once a girl he'd spend a lot of time with, Jasmin Straight—on marital leave from a psychiatrist elsewhere in New York, but going back —had been sharp enough to notice, and they had spent an afternoon making up fake examples of these blurtings out, for both her and him, and guessing at them in turn. "Bill made" turned out to be the day she had charged an expensive dress to her husband, and first cuckolded him; "Blood Soy" was when he thought of Vietnam in a Chinese restaurant. But when Jasmin got out of bed, tucking her chin in her chest in mock of him, she'd leaned over him with a last one she wouldn't explain. "Uh-uh, too worthy a guilt." Though he took her back to bed, he never wormed it out of her.

He was home now. Where the non-repetition of people in his life could still so worry him, the way they jogged companionably alongside, or intensely, then vanished only to reappear—in the African shadows of a dream, a plain American face mask-hanging—or in daytime memory a Tenniel cat in the trees. The worst was when you saw the face within a strange face, as he had seen Jasmin's once. But he had a vow that if he were ever to meet again any of these discards that had been winnowed out of the catalogue, it would have to be by the chance that would then *be* destiny. He would never call Jasmin up. Even though he still wanted to believe that, beginning with the beginning—after that he would take it on trust—his fate would be to re-encounter them all.

He saw Buddy at the gate, feeling his own pride in him. Little fellow you'd never catch wearing elevator shoes. Or those two-hundred-dollar elephant-hide ones either. The car that drew up for them had a chauffeur in it, but wasn't a limousine. Since Buddy had become an investment broker without leaving off being a lawyer, and had subsequently become a consultant without leaving off being a broker—after which Bunt was unsure of the details except that Buddy would never leave anything behind—his father had taken on the style of business money with real money, wherever this saved him time, but always kept the style subservient—like making

63

the chauffeur-hire give him a smaller car. And he had never been persuaded—how Maeve had tried!—to make his success physical to himself.

Sitting by his father on the familiar way in from Kennedy, his excitement grew; this time he knew why. The city demanded conclusions of him. False or true didn't matter; he'd lived in sight of its demands all his life. First came the blind warehouses, black with the dirt of years, full of mysterious industrial guilts heaped in wood and slag and zinc. Then came the flat-topped houses of people who worked there, and lived in streets out of a policeman's gazette. Then the newer factories, in whose clean halls the plastics refined themselves out of the living air, leaving behind a smell of Faust. A knot of viaducts, then old kiosks placarded with damp, then a spray of rumbling bridge over a slime of water. There, over there, the bristle of leafage and stone that had always been the Manhattan side. Scarabs of slum; then gradually that burden lessened. They were approaching the East Sixties; a mile north were the blocks where he had once been an Ambassador. Though they weren't going that far, even here the family sense was already strong. Maeve scrubbing city out of her neck with a nailbrush every evening. Buddy's collar wilting with it the big morning he went to borrow a stake from the bank. The city was against your finding it irresistible. And it was anti-memory too. Like some sporting, sparring uncle who slapped you on the mended collarbone saying *"That* where I hit you, boy?"

"There's the Manhattan Eye and Ear."

"Yeah, you had your tonsils out there. Maeve took you without telling you first." Buddy'd always resented this for him.

Calm and self-knowing, a nurse whose hidden white smell was still with him now, had sat down gripping him between her knees, and held out under his chin the paper cup of the terrible, thick stuff. Milk of magnesia, nothing. He knew it came from her. But he got it down, the white potion that made you mad or loved, lame or invulnerable. It was the dram you had to drink.

"From Central Park West. All the places we moved, Buddy. Do you ever mind?" Travel had made him blunter. Or his whole situation.

His father folded his arms, like a man who recalls he has soft parts to protect. He glanced at the chauffeur's barrier, as if the man out there could hear. "Hardest part is the philanthropy. You have to give to the opera, so you *go* to the opera."

Even with this, when they drew up on Fifth Avenue he still hadn't understood what his father was trying to say. Though the new building, new not just to them, had black marble bays bucking out of its white—as if the builder had dreamed of Byzantine while at the dentist, and the canopy was a gold-braided and draped palanquin you could scarcely emerge from with propriety unless you were on a horse—to him it was still only an apartment house. He did note that inside their state uniforms, the doormen were worse types every year.

65

In the elevator, Buddy said "Maeve's parties are still the same, Bunt. But I should warn you. She thinks this one's for you."

He nodded. They were at their floor. "Wow. One apartment to a floor. The Bronstein floor?"

Buddy nodded. There was a careworn look that some businessmen put on whenever their expenditure pointed to their own successes; he had never done that: his sadnesses would be his own. He brightened. "Jesus, I forgot." He took out two yarmulkas. "Found these in my chifforobe." Solemnly, they donned them, then broke up. "Congratulations, kid. Glad you're home." They shook hands.

"How's Maeve?" His chin dropped to his chest. What a sod he was, to wait until now to ask.

A shrug. The same complicitous one his grandfather used to exchange with the other men before they went into Sunday dinner, after conversations which were over a child's head. He could smell the yellow fricassee, and hear the uncles. The shrug that Jewish men made before they went in to join the women.

"I don't rock the boat." Buddy took out a bunch of keys, then thought better of it and rang, his head held high. Family life was a magnetic tape on which you were pulled along, hearing through walls maybe, but never speaking the ultimate—the process should not be disturbed.

Two locks were needed here, and a buzzer went off before a maid appeared—so ethnic she looked Eng-

66

lish to him—took his father's coat, scanned him for one, and left on the double, as if they were both strangers. Always before, he had been introduced. The postmistress in Wales, would she gawp now—or know how to spell this too? The Bronsteins had been on the up again while he was away; it had been that way each time he stood in front of a new door. One could have programmed the whole thing years ago; use his parents as the knowns—how well he knew them!—and a stipulated equation for the money rise, and get your answer. Here.

Idly he wondered what kind of trip Maeve was on now. He no longer cared about his room, though he knew there would be one. Europe had cured him of room-keeping, as even school never had; to the last there he had cherished his pinups, and a mock-up of Rockefeller Center he had made of construction paper and dried fishbone. But now the Bronsteins could do what they wanted with his corner of them. He had an architecture in his head now that wouldn't go away, plus all those penny-weights of knowledge that might come in handy someday; his head was now his house.

Oh, so we're richer, we're that kind of rich now, was all he thought, shedding his bag just inside the door on a floor that wasn't wood or even marble but some kind of inlaid brick. Real old brick, on second glance, Italian again. How did it feel here, transported like him, but begun and fabricated somewhere else?

"What's that?" A long black construct, like orange crates gone crenellated Moorish, but with some elusive presence that organized it out of junk—perhaps a bat or mouse that lived in it. "Why Bud—isn't that a Nevelson?"

"Bought it for the office opening. But when we placed the really big piece of hardware—the Zebel thing—Zebel wouldn't have it near. Said it detracted." Buddy shrugged. "I love her stuff, to me it looks like Brooklyn. But I just buy the tax deductions; against these art-boys who am I? And against Zebel. So I persuaded your mother the Nevelson would look better here than some Merovingian hatrack." They exchanged grins. Bronstein took off his tarboosh and hung it on one black spire, with what he thought was flair.

"Go ahead, why not?" his father said. "You know her father ran a lumberyard in Rockland, Maine? Now that's what I call artistic development."

And already twice today, that Maine had come up. But you couldn't depend on it—that in the end, everything in a life would.

In an anteroom all mirrors—Maeve had always loved these, but had never attained octagons before—he stopped short. "Mother came to the office?"

A yarmulka had never looked right on Buddy's middle-aged Manhattan-sharpie haircut, over his oyster-white, too-silky ties. Now, with the hair longer, even though smartly grayed by some barber, and in spite of one of those wide ties, by some designer who had been on Turkish *kif* maybe, it blended in.

"Once she did. Once."

"How come?"

"For the opening. You didn't see the papers? I had Blum send clips. No—of course." The yarmulka nodded, sideways, in the old style; it did have an influence. "The Mayor came, the Arts Council people too. A lot of, you know—*people.*" Buddy looked down his own length, always a sign of modesty. "I do a little work for things like the Odyssey House—dope rehabilitation you know—and certain other *city* questions. Prisons, land-marks even—" He flashed a kinship smile. "I keep out of the arts, except to give." He sighed. "That opera. ...And to buy. But any other city question, they know I'll go for it. From your grampa I get it, maybe—remember his wayward boys?"

"Sure do."

They had come in their Sunday suits from the orphanage or the reform school, and his grandfather had taken them to the ballgame. Limp hands in Bun-ty's—they seemed not to know how to shake it—and flinty eyes on him and his house. Or scared ones. He knew that look, from the PS before PS 6. They were afraid they weren't to be trusted. There was always such a progression of them; that was the trouble. One had lasted long enough in his grandfather's esteem for the boy to be given a job, but it hadn't worked out.

"How'd it work out down there? With Maeve?"

"So-so. No, not good, why should I lie to you? She looked beautiful, absolutely. Your mother's still a—" His father smeared two fingers over an eye and stretched his mouth. "But it doesn't seem to help. Sit down, boy. Sit down."

69

He sat on a satin bergère, on the edge.

Through his father's account, he saw the whole scene: the reception line, the photographer's fireworks.

"She hostessed it all just fine, just as if she hadn't walked in cold on the arrangements, but had done it all herself. Cool she was, like born to it. And I thought, now I've got it for her, it's all turned out right. She even posed with Mrs. Blum."

His father's secretary, from way back when. Whom Maeve had displaced. Who had again taken Maeve's place. What a continuity, now that one thought of it.

"Then some confounded girl reporter—big tall girl with a shiv in her purse instead of a pen—asked her if she hadn't been my secretary, once. And I could see it begin to fall apart." His father leaned into one of the mirrors as if he was seeing it there. "Once again." Buddy smoothed his shave, clenched a fist and rested his chin on it, wide-eyeing himself in the glass—there was a picture of him in that posture as a newsboy, in knickers and shouldersack. "I shouldn't have started that secretary joke with her, years ago. When a person hurts, and you keep rubbing it in—maybe it all started with that secretary joke."

"I don't buy that."

"You don't? Bunty, wanna know something? Neither do I. But the psychiatrist does."

"She going to one?"

"No. Mine."

"You? What do you need a—"

70

"Thanks, pal. Because she wouldn't. Better than nothing, they said. She's in a bad state of equilibrium."

He hung back, then. Why was his father hanging back? "Will I find her—changed?"

"No, son." His father said it mildly. "Just the same." He got up suddenly. "Say Bunt, take a look through here."

His father was applying his left eye to what looked like a metal-rimmed hole in one of the mirrors.

"What is it?"

"No secrets, no more secrets." Buddy applied the other eye to the hole. "Came with the house. A spyglass. From room-to-room. The public ones. First I thought I'd block them off; now I can't do without. Who's ever at the party I wanna bypass, I can. Right up to my room. Take a look."

He saw a room in reverse opera-glass scale, at first only the floor. The device had a swivel, and a lens adjuster, very clever. There was nobody in the next room.

"Your room's on the same line as mine. Next to the armory."

"Armory?"

"The guy was a military buff. Wanna wash up?"

"No thanks." He couldn't resist though. "What's it like?"

"Living like this? Aren't I used?"

"My room."

"Not so bad, you know. She gave a lotta thought."

Eagle Eye

"Hell. I won't be staying, Buddy."

"She knew that, Bunty. She knew that. I'll tell you what it's like. It's like a room in an Italian hotel."

His father closed the little round door of the spyhole, wiped its mirror with a handkerchief. You could hardly see it was there. "Smart, always so smart, isn't she?" Buddy said. "When I pushed about the doctor. 'What'll he tell me—' she says. 'That I'm a quick learner? Who learns only dreck?' . . . Excuse me, Bunty—you understand that language?"

He'd forgotten his father's delicacy with a son's other half. "Why not? She does."

"Dreck. That an Irish girl should learn only that from us. From New York."

"Why New York?" It burst from him. "Why not from Amenia?"

At once—echoes. Blaming the suburbs. He smiled to himself. Hadn't thought of Witkower in a long time.

"You think? You think?"

"Now I remember, Buddy—" he said, grinning "—whenever you have one of those things on your head, you start talking like Gramps."

"*Right*. City College drops from me like a *lei*." His father took off the embroidered circle, smoothed it. "Or maybe because I went back to Amenia, *enn wye*. A while back, Bunt. She was so low. I thought—up there's the only audience Maeve ever wanted; maybe I never tried hard enough to get it down here."

"You tried. Lots of times."

"I never went down on my knees before. Catholics

72

love the knee position." He folded the yarmulka and put it in his pocket. "Brace yourself, Bunty, your Granma's here."

"Mother MacNeil?"

"Herself. Her winsome self and all her broomsticks. She finally sold the farm. She had it up for sale for a long time."

"Sold it, huh." He'd like to think of it there, regardless.

Quentin smiled at him. "To me. Oh she doesn't know that. Through an agent. Yeah. I worked hard."

"And mother—how did she—?"

"With *her* mother? Oh Maeve hated the idea—gave her something to live for. That's when we moved here—remember?"

"Sort of." He recalled a letter, that must have been asking him if he wanted to come to the office gala, though Quentin hadn't called it that, or even made quite plain that it was an invite. Said letter, and its successor reminding him to write to the office until they got settled—because he hadn't written at all, of course—had been left behind on the washbasin of a convenience hotel in Montmartre; he remembered the basin very well, and the girl he'd picked up at the American Express—a last resort—and had spent a day with her until he tipped she was on speed. Streaking around the room after him like a candidate for Dracula: "Sure, I'm still Algiers-nutty; when it's gone I'll lay off. Done it before." He'd had a time getting her down. Bundled in her ski-cap and cape, she looked as pink and princess-faced as when

73

they met. "Being in the skin always sets me off, though. Ta-ta, Bunny." She went off to meet her folks, who were picking her up to see Paris with them, before college. She never did get his name right, which had annoyed him. And now he couldn't dig up hers.

"But that was only three months ago, Bud." He looked down at the bergère he was sitting on, the mirrors, outlined in gold gesso, that reflected it, and him. Since first in Europe, he had begun to look. "Even for Maeve—this is some place to get together."

"Oh no, we bought it lock, stock and barrel, we did practically nothing. Wasn't time. Well—let's move on."

They went through a couple of rooms that resembled the old first one of their succession of places on Park—or what that one had been modeled on. Cooled down too, but older, and more windows—arched.

"A harpsichord!" The family pictures on it, his father's parents and collaterals, were in silver now; he remembered which place that happened in—the first East Side one, off Madison. But the last place, the one he'd left them in, some three blocks east of here, was pretty much of a blank.

Buddy patted the instrument on its flower-painted case. "Came with. Two others, we sold off."

"Some shopping spree."

"That was the idea." Buddy stopped square under a pink-and-green china chandelier that flew and stopped at the same time, like a hunk of Mozart. "Wasn't that—always the idea?"

All this confidence they had kept from him, now must he have it in one big wad? To make a man of him?

"Will you move again?"

"Where?" His father swept the keyboard from top to bottom. No sound came out of it. It was a mute. Or else had to be pumped. Buddy looked mollified. "No. No more moving. A family ought to be hemmed in."

It all sounded like shit. A world-dwarfing—the kind families picked. "It works with Maeve, then. Having— G-Granma—here."

Buddy was picking up the photos, putting them down again, one by one. "We forget, kid. Audiences don't wait."

Mother MacNeil had had a stroke two days after getting here. "Maybe a compliment," Buddy said. "Anyway, know all these nasty or stupid-looking old women in winghats and wheelchairs get walked around this neighborhood by some sweetfaced colored woman—I don't know why but they always both are—well we're in that class now too. Only Mother made clear, even with her whole left side paralyzed, that she doesn't like blacks. So we have a broken-down gen- tlewoman—think that's what you'd call her—instead. Think that's what you *will* call her." Buddy gave him a meaningful smirk he didn't get. "If you weren't a grown man, we could have a governess even. And the family would be complete . . . Well, here's the dining room. We haven't eaten here yet."

And no wonder. Bunty put down the safari bag he'd dragged with him. "Wh—when will you start."

"Today. All for you, Bunty-boy."

"It looks like—like the monk's refectory on Mount Athos."

"Where's that?"

"A monastery. Greek. On an island. Where no women can come, not even hens."

"So?"

"This place where we ate." But not so fake brown-gaunt, so fake bare as this. And not so big. It was the long table reminded him. He should have said the Cloisters. If he'd seen that tapestry in time, hanging on the bouldered wall like a muffled report from Art History I, he would have said it. For he could tell that he and Buddy, with all else shared—even at Maeve's cost—had all of a sudden reached a low. Their lowest since he got here. Maybe because it was at Maeve's cost, his father had now reneged. Anyway, for his son to show off his foreign medals, when Buddy, no fool, so delicate—he could feel it—had been offering him his confidence!

He gobbled something to his chest—no time to find out what.

Buddy's nostril twitched—had he been onto Bunt's habit long since? No, his eyes had what Maeve called his Ellis Island look. Greenhorn. Even Gramps had had it sometimes. "Monasteries. You go for them?"

"Just a place I went." Irritated. Wrong. Slowly his boot-toe circled a floorboard wide as a modest coffin. The groined ceiling was like a cloister, only insufferably hot. His raw-wool shirt still smelled of its lanolin. Maybe his father had meant him to wash. If I stink like a sheep, he could say, it's just Wales and emotion. Truly. Truth came out of him. "I g-guess, huh—we must be pretty rich."

Gawp. He could have picked nothing worse. He watched his father grind a fist on the table, turn sharply, and march to the window, where he turned his back—a family trait when agitated. A Bronstein trait like the shibboleth his son had just stepped on. For a Bronstein, money was only the game behind the dream. Gramps, a CPA turned actuary, and always as much interested in other peoples' incomes and probabilities as in his own, had drawn a stiff line between what you could do for money and what you must do with it—particularly for "those of our race" who had got past the starvation line with any sort of bounce. Maeve's side of Bunty was resignedly accepted and given over to the women—who both took care of the assimilation that had to be in the new country, and took the blame for it. Exposure of what you had was the sin—the more you had. Every Sunday that Bunty sat with the men before dinner Grandfather had reached out of the endless conversation at some point to put a hand on his head for emphasis. "Bunty, be a Montefiore, not a Rothschild." Not many of the family had adhered to this high standard, either way. Buddy, the youngest son, whom the eager, hawk-nosed females had belatedly named Quentin—"in 1925!" for Teddy Roosevelt's dead hero-son—had done his best.

"You boys, you slop around Europe, running around all the circles we left it for—what do you know?" Buddy turned round, choked on his fury, yellow with it, clutching the curtain behind him. Whenever he grew fat and waxy, he dieted himself thin, until the newsboy's face sat on his fifty-year-old shoulders. And had his blood run through all sorts of purifications, and returned to him—maybe not for health alone. "Knapsacking around, never coming home, God forbid we should die and who do we notify—*poste restante*? A street address two weeks old, in Bombay? In Holland a nightclub—who goes to nightclubs in Holland? And once in a while—lucky lucky—the American Express . . . What do you know about it all?"

"About what, Buddy?" He knew the question well. Asked of himself at every address.

"About *life* in this country. About what goes on here, has to be done here."

"Compromises?" He could never raise his voice to match Buddy's. Maybe only fathers could manage it. He thought of Tarzan.

"About what"—Buddy's voice sank to a wheeze. "About what can be *done* in this country." His eyes bulged; he was tallying it. Opera houses. Prisons. Landmarks. Wayward boys.

78

A swinging door opened. A capped maid peered in to see what the rumpus was. Buddy waved her back, with a drowning gesture. The door closed.

"Maybe you forgot, Dad, hmm. Did you? Why I left."

Homerun. How quickly the honeybrown, money-brown eyes went wet, covered themselves with a hand.

He could hear murmurs in the kitchen. To one side of the tapestry there was one of those portholes. He crossed the floor to peer in, seeing only black, but waiting for Buddy to compose his face. When he did turn, Buddy was toeing the safari bag. "Still got it, huh."

He crossed the floor and stood beside him, nodding. Carry it everywhere. It's my life.

Lips tucked in, they nodded at each other with the barely perceptible orbit of mourners. But it was also as if his father, hands clasped, was worshipping him.

Yes, I'm your riches, your only. You helped hide me, or would have. What can an idol not made of stone say to you?

"Papa. You want me to wash?"

His room on the second floor was so like the hotel, his foot stopped at the door, as if another step would sink him deep in a cloud. A matter of wood that was

79

old and marble that was cheap, how had she caught that plain, sweet meagerness, even here? Of a room privy to anything, but in-the-faith. She hadn't imitated any one thing, and she had remembered to include Marlene's old bureau. There was no more bookspace, though, than at Montecatini—a small ledge. She knew he couldn't stay. The room told him what she had observed. Was meant to. When a man keeps telling a woman she's smart, he wondered, when does she catch on he means smart *but,* even if he doesn't know it yet? From the first?

A few minutes later, he and Buddy, standing on a balcony overlooking the main hall—you had to call it a hall—were still avoiding her. To do so together was a comfort, and therefore worse. He put his head down and muttered something.

"What?" Buddy said.

"Oh, nothing." He had caught his own words just in time, always unnerving. *Comforts are aging*—Jasmin would have laughed. "Who built this place, some dictator?" Two steps more and they could look down unseen, from a prayer-corner torn from some church.

"Dunno. Man I bought it from was a former tenor at the Met. See those spotlights in the ceiling? Work out fine for the art." Buddy coughed. There was pride here.

"Rothko's, are they? And Clifford Still." Down below, each panel glowed like a looking-glass entrance to a provence just behind it. Or an exit.

"You know about them, huh. What do you know!"
Buddy held out his hand. "Sorry kid. What I said. Go
round the world again, you want to."

"Please." Button up.

"Right. But we won't move from here. You can
depend on it."

What a place to stop. Even the pictures want out.

"Some South American had the place before that.
The original owner, I don't know."

People should save those things. There ought to
be a bank for it.

"Gangsters maybe? Al Capone, that period? Those
peepholes." The niche they were standing in came from
a church, maybe forty years back. It would be an interesting place to take a girl.

"Bunt, the whole place went up only five years ago."

"Wuddya know." Already he was talking like Buddy.
"Well, let's not lurk."

"I don't see your mother down there. Maybe she's
in the terrarium."

"Where's that?"

"We couldn't put it on the Avenue side. Around
the corner, on the court. Even for that, we had to have
a variance." He cast Bunt a look. "I've had to take an
interest. More and more."

There were about fourteen people down there, wan-
dering party-style, their heads vulnerable to any boy
on a viaduct. He saw that it was old party-style, twos
and threes. No clusters, nobody on the floor. A grouty

Eagle Eye

homesickness jumped him from behind and hung on him like an ape-girl, from that world of fur pillows, jack-in-the-beanstalk boots, cavalier hair, and music cuffing the neck like a steady training partner, which he had made for and hit in any town in Europe. If he turned his head, he would surely see her topaz lantern-eyes, blubbery from the smoke-tickle. A lovely gorilla girl, with a look of Jane Fonda about her little nose. Then she would get off his back, and turn into maybe a girl in a shabby greatcoat with a pile like rinsed feathers —Clara Rentschle, Dutch girl working for Air France as an airport-meeter for middle-aged Americans who liked to be shoe-horned into their hotels—saying "You're new to Lipps. Care to join us in a *kir*?" And the town would begin.

Trouble was, he didn't want to go back. He wanted it to begin here.

"Maybe Maeve doesn't want to see us." Or me.

From as far back as summer camp, they had always written jointly, the same couple of pages, rambling over the sparse facts, and full of their dependable duty to *him*.

"Come on. I just told her a later plane, so we could have our talk."

"Do I see a couple of *priests* down there?"

A wheelchair, containing a clawy little creature in a church hat, was being pushed toward the pair by a figure in blue. No Maeve.

82

"Only two? Soon they'll send the army. Bunt, I should warn you. You're the one really bought this place."

"Me? Gramp's policy? You're kidding." A twenty-year endowment for $10,000, payable on his majority. In the load of insurance Buddy had mortgaged for his stake, that had been the only one left out. Thanks kid, it won't help.

"My sacred promise to the old lady. To get her down here."

"You don't mean you promised? That we'd convert?" After the funeral visit, there'd been a breath of it. If they'd send him up there to St. Joseph's-in-the-Valley, Mother MacNeil would board the New York orphan, as well as reform him. Cut her Mother's throat first, Maeve said.

"Me, they're satisfied if I go back to being a good Jew. The church is very liberal these days. You're the tender morsel they're hungry for."

"Sonofa gun."

"So I'm a rascal. Allow me, once."

They were both grinning.

"How do I know I brought you up right? I have my guilts."

"You know I've never been anything. You took advantage of it."

"What a thing to say, you're a nothing. No, I only took advantage you're young. It's your turn now."

"Jesus, what a birthday present."

"You want the farm?" Swiftly. "You can have it. I won't sell it, then."

Canny canny. He turned on his heel in the prie-dieu, puzzling.

"Mother MacNeil loves it up here. Brings up her portable Virgin every day."

Maybe the old Brooklyn money-fear wasn't so false. Deuces wild, the money says to you. You have a fantasy?—act it out. You can move. You're not hemmed in.

"I'll h-have a cow, maybe."

"Fine. She'll look just right in that dining room."

"Well, let's go down, huh." He took his father's arm, as height permitted. "Maybe they'll make a man of me."

"Of us," Buddy said.

On the bottom step, he stopped. "What are they doing about Maeve?"

His father held up his newsboy face. "For her—they pray."

The two of them had to get all the way down the stairs to see all of it before he understood what had happened to the Bronsteins, and how rich they were. Anybody who had been reared in his collection of angles, walls, views, courtyard-juttings that almost provided the city-coveted "double exposure," fire escapes that did at last bring the morning sun—a whole mute storehouse of wistful accommodation—could be excused for thinking it.

84

The Fifth Avenue side was all glass—so much of it, and so clean, it seemed all air. Maybe angels came and licked it in the early morning—Paulina Vespasi again, telling him why the Chrysler Building's needle always shone so clean, "same as the Vittorio Emmanuele monument." And the air curved and wrapped itself nonchalantly, accepting a roofline, but dispensing with smaller privileges. Outside there, the whole upper city offered itself at sunset-level, no cover-charge, a gorgeous cloud-cafeteria for all bums. Strain for more meaning at your own risk. In case of too much ardor, on the terrace beyond the windows there were parapets.

To the left, where the building curved in, an open door—yes, that was air, like summer on his boots—gave on a striped party-marquee and all the fixings, white tables and spots of chrysanthemum bushes, stacked against the dusk. He had no trouble believing they were real. There were even a couple of girls in front of the nearest bush. I see you, he signaled to himself. I'll get back to you. Stay there.

To his right, on the far north corner, about fourteen feet back from the angle, he saw the terrarium, a bulb of opaline glass perhaps ten feet in diameter, extruded on air again, as if the building had blown a last bubble before it gave up its climb. Outside a just-perceptible sliding-door, a life-sized porcelain lion raised its chub head. Inside, all the shapes of hothouse-green pressed lovingly toward him. They wanted to get in here, why was that? In their center, behind lattice, vine and spike,

85

a life-sized statue with its back turned—the old Kwan-Yin from Park Avenue Two, its ivory coif bent, looking out. Clever.

No, it's Maeve.

You must know, Betts, that she was absolutely lucid. Perhaps more absolutely lucid than she had to be. Her only aberration was that she had to go into that place once an hour—not on the hour, nothing so bald as that—and gaze down. Whatever was being looked at there, the former owners of such vantage points as tree-houses, captain's walks and pergolas—or a small porch in the Berkshire past—are not required to say.

She tripped out of there, not seeing him at first, in the same white wool dress and bronze shoes he and Buddy had had to applaud over and over before she could trust herself to wear them to his graduation, an event she had trained for—as she did for all public appearances outside their house, and some in it—as if she were a movie star. "There'll be so many bigwig parents there." Though nothing ever came of that for her—she always became ashamed of the impudence that had brought her thus far, and hung back inside the shell she had made to be looked at—he had been proud of her, when he saw some of the other boys' old bags. And Buddy had afterwards lunched downtown with one of the fathers, who in a whisper to his own son, had asked to be introduced to him.

As his mother came toward him, seeing her now, it was hard to believe she was not a girl. Since he'd last seen her, she must have given up "keeping up the red" of her hair. It was now a silvery white, brushed high off her face and clipped at the back George Washington-style, in an exaggerated version of half the girls he knew—why should going white make her look like a girl? Thanks to the procession of them between her and him, he could wonder now if she had a lover— something in the way she looked over her shoulder and away from him—looking back:

"Welcome to your party," she cried toward him.

There were people about; this was for their benefit. He understood her need of falsity, compact between them since their shopping days.

She fell upon him then, saying the archly natural thing. "Where's your beard?"

"Left it with a friend."

Maeve tapped his shoulder. A little smile. "Mick mouth."

87

Eagle Eye

His heels were bumped from behind.

"Sor-ree!" Too loud to be.

He turned. Wheelchair croquet. The woman who was manning it shed him a hard-nosed glare from behind her navy-blue. Same as the mothers in the park: babies take precedence. Or because *they* had to be with the carriage all day. And you were with a girl.

"Mother, this is Bunty," Maeve said. "He's been in Wales."

He took the little claw, half afraid it would scratch. Under her blanket, Mother MacNeil still looked like a cat they had talcumed over very neatly, and put a hat and bunioned shoes on. Her black wrinkles matched her coat.

"She can understand you, but you have to bend down," the attendant said. "She must have been a little deaf even before. Lip-reads a little." She bent down. "*Wales.* He's been in *Wales.*"

The old woman struggled to speak. Said something.

"Learning to talk." His mother said quietly. "That's the day I leave."

"For shame, Maeve." The attendant had a champagne glass in one hand. Whose companion was she?

"You remember Mrs. Reeves," Buddy said behind him.

"Buddy was so generous, bringing Mother here," Maeve said at Buddy. "I thought I'd be generous back."

He squinted, removing himself. They had never used him like this, or had they. Maeve was looking down

—her bronze buckles. Her shoes never showed wear. She wouldn't look at him.

Old Reeves's white hair had been dyed brown. A little of her backbone had gone with it. Or into the wheelchair.

"I had a mother once," Mrs. Reeves said. "For a very—*hic*—long time."

The light was pretty here. Acknowledge it. Not a cathedral light, but the old chemical stain gathered anywhere there was a roof and a dusk. Not to be spent with old people. A waiter came up and changed their glasses, each full of light. Mother MacNeil was given a sip too. Their four faces looked at him hopefully. Yes, Bunty, this is how rich we are.

"Oops, she wants to write something." Reeves bent to his grandmother. "Well, off we go. She won't—except in the bathroom. Isn't that extraordinary? Most people read."

"Well, I'm off to my party. I see two possible love-objects over there." He touched his mother's arm. "Watch my line, anyone?"

"Excuse me a minute. Take your father. He never knows many people here."

Buddy and he watched her open a door in the terrarium and disappear among the plants.

"When a depression gets very low, Bunt, people say anything they think. The doctor says."

"Wuddya know, I do it without thinking."

He would have to cheer them up.

In succession, he took three fast tries.

A yellow-haired man came up, and was introduced to him as the designer of the terrarium.

"Claes Hilversum here—haven't we met somewhere?"

"You Dutch? El Paradiso, maybe, I used to hang out there."

"That government place? No, I have not been. I have not been a student for some years." This was no exaggeration. "Cheapest pot in Europe, though, I hear." He took out a wildly elegant case and angled it. "Have some."

Bunty handed Buddy his glass. "Hold my bottle." He and the blond boy, so called, lit up.

"Morocco?" Claes said, breathing close. "Rue de l'Art? Leuwenstrasse? Lapses like that bawthair me. We must talk."

"The M-Mowzel," Bunt said quickly. He turned to Buddy. "English for mousehole." Handed Claes back his joint. "That place in Soho, with a—with a suit of armor takes your hat."

"R-right," Claes said. "What a lovely idea."

"We had a place with a suit of armor, once, remember Buddy? Central Park West."

He and Buddy exchanged smiles. In the foyer, like a truant from the lobby, sent to guard them with its pike. One of the cousins, asking its price, had scolded, "Maeve, you could have a mink coat for that." His mother's report of this had become family-famous between the three of them, Buddy teasing for years. At the time Bunty hadn't understood why. Suspecting his mother didn't either, quite. "Imagine," she'd said that night at dinner. "Imagine anybody wanting a mink coat. When you could have a suit of armor."

Maeve, just returning, slipped under Bunty's arm. The way she smiled, she understood it now. "The armor? Wish we still had it. I could put it in the terrarium."

"Why?" Keep it going, if you can't cheer.

"She'd like to put everything in there," Buddy said. "Last week that little safe with the jewelry. Thought it would be a swell place for it. And this week, another load of plants."

They'd bought the jewel-safe, an imposing many-drawered affair, in the gift shop, their first trip on the Michaelangelo—the most expensive item there. Since then Buddy put something into it any anniversary handy; it must be crammed. Mostly with the diamonds she was indifferent to—"I always feel I'm only boarding them." There was also the pale Ceylon ruby she'd told the cousins was a tourmaline, more gold junk she never wore, and the small pearls which were her emblem. She had them on now, hung with the opal she did love, and called her bad-luck-piece.

Was it crazy to keep that stuff out there? Or smart? Claes puffed irritated smoke at her, from a straight cigarette. "I told you. That drome is built for a lifetime—all right, all right. But to a certain stress."

"You said we could even dance in it."

"So you can—I've built twenty-five of them. They respond to motion in the usual way. And take any reasonable bearing weight. But they have an overload point like anyplace." He turned to Bunty, flashing teeth. "Like those waterbeds in your old brownstones here, too dangerous, don't you agree?" And to Buddy. "This is the first attached to poured concrete. Give me the key, Maeve, will you. I'd better check."

She unhitched a dainty one, fitted somehow on her belt.

They watched him unlock. The doorcurve couldn't be distinguished from the rest. Copied from Bucky Fuller, he would guess. Beautifully executed. "Why lock it?"

"Doughty pries in there and lifts a leg," his father said. "Part of the floor's earth."

New dog, then. "Must be some dog."

They could see a vague outline of Claes inside, bending and touching. Funny how anything inside there looked as if it were struggling to get out.

Claes came back, handing Maeve the key. "Looks all right, I must say. New plants look groggy, better feed them. See you did take out the Chinese porcelains. Bulls and lions your mother had in there, Bunty. And a Kwan Yin. Terrible example of one. Like a diplomat in drag."

"I miss her company." Maeve touched her own hair. "She's in a nearby closet, though. And the safe, Buddy. I took out that."

"Where'd you put it?"

"Sent it to the office. Care of Blum."

"To Blum? What did you do that for?"

"Not *to* her, Buddy. Care of. Isn't that what secretaries are for?"

His mother had a style now, he saw, wincing. The temporary-starvation style that girls got when they went thin.

"Well, ta-ta all," Claes sighed. "God, I do beautiful work. You see the piece on it in *Art News* —'L'art nouveau *nouveau*'? Sure you don't want to back me, Mr. Bronstein? I'd love to be a Limited. Or even an Inc."

"No thanks, Claes, I told you. This way it stays art. That way—you're only a supplier."

"What a fate. Well, nice to have met you again, Bunty, we must get together."

"See you at the Mowzel."

"That lovely place. But we needn't go so far." He slouched across the room to a Rothko, slid the panel aside, and slipped out. Buddy watched, scowling.

"I think he has an effeminate interest in you, Bunt."

He was touched. Buddy could be as naive as Maeve. "Not to worry."

"Where'd *that* come from?"

"It's English. Like the Mowzel."

"What's the Mowzel?" Buddy said sullenly. "One of those haunts?"

"I made it up."

Maeve laughed.

93

A bad pause then. Why should that be? Maybe they weren't looking to him to cheer them. Maybe the dog did it now.

"Chickie, Bunt," his father said suddenly. "Here come the cops."

The two priests were coming their way.

"You sicked 'em on me." Wasn't like his father, to play both ends through the middle. He reached up and slid the yarmulka, still on his own head, forward and sideways. Half and half.

"Father Melchior, my son Quentin," Maeve said. Quentin. Was she so impressed with the cloth after all, then? Or only with the father himself, a huge man with an oversized, fresco face. She looked inquiringly up at the other one. "Father always brings us somebody new."

"Archie Dunham, ma'am," the second one said, looking down even on Bunty, from an elegant, yellow-skinned face that sat like a finial on his seven-foot bones. "But I reckon your son and I already know each other."

This time it was true. "You were graduating the year I came." He'd been the basketball star at Bunt's last prep school. And their star black. "You ordained already?"

"Seminarian. Like you?"

"What? Oh, you mean my hat? Just my at-home hat. You know, like a smoking jacket."

"Smoke?" Archie offered his pack.

"Thanks, I don't." He laughed at himself, and up

94

at Archie, much too hard. How explain his elation? Fancy meeting you, anybody, here. Maybe the town had begun.

"You were swimming team, weren't you?"

"Second string."

"Hear you're going to be an architect," Father Melchior put in. "I was a curator before I took orders. In Denmark. Hear you been in Bruges and Amsterdam. See any of my favorite churches? See St. Sauveur?"

Clearly they knew everything about him. Maybe Archie had even been *sent*.

"No, guess I only saw girls." He reached out to touch Buddy's arm. "Not to worry."

He took advantage of the pause. "One I knew in London, her father wrote a history of the Vatican." Why did he always feel he had to talk Catholic to Catholics?

"I think I *know* that book" Melchior said. "Came out in the fifties. And of the author. Very old family in the church, they are. Since Henry the Eighth."

"Uh-huh. Lots of yummy childhoods, they talk about."

They'd talked about hers all night, in the family house on the edge of Paddington. With her, it had been like foreplay; every time he touched a further zone, some old nurse or old goody gardener had jumped out. None of her family was home though, and toward dawn, when she'd been finishing a raunchy tale of what the girls had once dreamed up at St. Hilda's, he'd had reasonable hopes. Then the family sheep dog had

95

walked in, a ringer for Peter Pan's, and the night was over. Always woke her for breakfast, the dear pet did—ever since she was a child.

"I think we use that book at the seminary," Archie said.

"Approved by the Vatican, I understand," Bunty said. "But banned in Ireland." He hadn't made that up, just retained it. Hopefully. He looked down. Maeve was gone again. It was like a tic.

For the second time he watched her take up the key at her waist, rest her hand on the knob for a moment, then enter, closing the door's perfectly bent line behind her, her shadow diffusing behind the plants. In that moment before, holding the knob, she bowed her head—could she be crossing herself? Once, on his own plea during a shopping day, she had taken him into St. Patrick's. During all the bobbing and ducking she hadn't done anything, only explained some of it to him. He had wanted to light a votive candle, but she wouldn't let him. Maybe her body remembered the old actions, vaguely repetitive. In time of need.

"Going to Ireland myself next year."

"Are you, Mr. Dunham?" Buddy was watching her too. "What'll you be doing there?"

"Serving, I hope." Archie looked modestly down. "At least neither side will mistake me for the other."

God, but he was token. "Uh-huh, easier than at basketball." At once, Bunty's head dropped his chest for shame, but this time nothing came out. He looked up to find Melchior observing him. "What are the s-stations of the Cross? I always wondered."

"Come by the rectory someday, why don't you, and I'll tell you." Melchior took pencil and pad out of a pocket and wrote the address for him. "By the way, your grandmother gave me this to give to you." He handed over a folded slip of lined paper. "Wonderful, how she is dealing with her infirmity."

He put it in his pocket unread. Mail of any kind meant obligation.

"Don't you want to read it?" the Dane said.

"Private," Bunty said. "She composes in the bathroom."

Buddy's shoulders shook—maybe this was what he had wanted of him. "Well excuse me—I must go round the other guests."

He went toward Maeve.

"Well, excuse me." Bunty said. "I promised to go back to those girls over there." Miracle, they were still together over there. "Bye, Archie. Keep the faith." He shook the Dane's big business-like hand. "B-bye, Mr. Melchior." Halfway across the room he blushed for that, but didn't look back.

"Place looks like Pompeii, doesn't it?" A passing voice said. Not to him: "the evening before."

He didn't turn round. His parents had always given parties that seemed born to be hostless. And were duly snubbed for it. He could see what the voice meant. The room he had crossed, on a tide of red carpet that had penetrated every corner like stage blood, had two mantels—one at either end—both of palely chased palace-marble. No fireplaces went with, but over one mantel hung a great toothy vagina, in whose sculped vortex a whole half of an ill-advised man could be received. In front of the other, a plaster-cast workman, whose lineaments were more true-to-life than flesh was, mused over a lunch-bucket under a Tiffany lamp. He felt that both sculptures were there to reassure him that the natural functions were all right. To his left, the huge abstracts stood about as required, like guests. Nudes would have looked awful here—classical. Loose usage of Pompeii though—to which Emilio had taken him, round the little rouged rooms, pale with fright, in which you could feel the owners, blown clear of luxury. "Look!" Emilio had said. "We still eat from a pot like that." Of pots that lasted like that, you could be proud.

Two women, taking champagne from the same tray a waiter offered him, were talking about the rug on top of the red carpet. "Handmade, wonder who?"

Toneless, asymmetric, it had been kept on since the second Park Avenue place, as a work of art. Nobody had ever copulated on it, far as he knew.

"V-vsoské," he said politely. A name to stick in the head. Like Silveira, the scrimshaw carver. Maeve's first suppliers, clubbily and constantly referred to, remained in his memory like habitués of the house.

The woman stared. "Over there. On the terrace." "Hmmm?"

"Thought you asked for whiskey."

He bowed, like the Polish Ambassador should, and walked toward it, pocketing his yarmulka on the way. Keeping his head down kept the voices disembodied.

"—compassionate." A male one. "Doctor says I have to be. Or else it's bad for me."

Fine, you do that. That's progress.

In a corner he shared the joke with his champagne.

Nobody had ever talked people here, much. One couldn't expect it. Jasmin said it wasn't done much any more in America, or even in New Zealand, where she came from. General attitudes and pursuits had taken over, like bombing and sports. Hoping for better, she had married a psychiatrist—but he was too old for it. And by profession a people-*changer*, which wasn't the same thing. The only people you could trust to be interested in themselves for themselves were the young, she said. Four years older than he, she was still cavalier about wrinkles, but watched herself like a movie for signs of mental age. "Pomp is the worst. It creeps." Bunty's tic would help save him, she said. The husband had told her to come back when she stopped confusing him with her ideas. "See the difference between him and ideas, he meant. He's never confused." Now and then she did go back. But inevitably, an idea cropped up.

"You don't do that with me," he'd said, looking round him for her ideas. Her place was one of the few he liked, as a place. Random. She was the kind of person other people gave stuffed animals to. That they wanted themselves. A largish kangaroo, brought by someone who had thought New Zealand was the same as Australia. Two small teddies, mating in dust, though the rest of the place was clean enough. A grass basket given her by someone at the archeological museum where she'd worked before coming here. Also a small framed drawing of what she said was a poisonous but very timid spider, called a katipo. And over the headboard a woodblock she had once bought, a scene of a rainy day, whose slanting rain-lines had to be well stared at before he saw these were words. All the same one.

She had a broad pansy-face, with almost invisible eyebrows that clenched exactly like that flower. "No, I don't, do I." She smiled up at him—a long, warm mold of small-print calico, pressed beneath him. Greenery-yallery, she called it. Almost all the girls that year had been wearing it. Last year. "I didn't say it, Bunt. You."

"I don't stick," he'd said to her sometime before that. "It's the way I move." He always said that to them carefully, not for brass but because it felt true. Never telling them how they all stuck, in the marvelous meat-packing larder that was his brain.

On the West Side Highway uptown, there was a butchers' warehouse with a runway open to the river, where you saw the men, the torsos and the meathooks, neat in the early morning. Once, passing there, he told her. How his girl-memories were all stacked up like that,

not murdered but treasured, because in the abattoir of
memory they were all the same one—to whom each time
he had said, "This is for once." The car had nearly
mounted Grant's Tomb with their laughter. "You save
us all?"—"Sure, no guilt. Because no heads." He didn't
tell her that this formal lineup took the place of all those
whom he hadn't expected life to take away from him.
He did explain that it had a permanence, or was achiev-
ing one. "So has Don Juan's," she said moodily, laughter
gone. They had a fight.

The most frightening thing is permanence, he tried
to tell her, not because you are locked in—but because
there isn't any. It must be we all want to be locked in.

They'd made up.

He was only thinking of calling her because he was
in America, and could call.

The terrace was as reassuring as an ad—nobody
on it but a butler looking morosely at his hands, who
snapped to at the sight of trade. And the two glossies.
How marvelously repetitive girl-types could be. He
already doted on that dent where the brownhaired one's
waist was, having often guided it over crosswalks,
squeezed it any number of situations, and lain with his
head in its concave. She had on an armless jerkin, pants,
a pouch at the waist, and a tan. A tan swimmer, she
would be, with a nice temper. The other girl's hair sil-
vered and spun on itself, with one little flip waiting to
be tugged; under it was the kind of dazzled eye and
loose lip-gleam that made her hard to focus on—there

was even a 1920's-in-Berlin look about her fuzzy dress and frappé color; she would be the one with whom you do anything. Inside her very possibly was a slum.

What fun it was. He was always wrong.

The air on terraces was always carbonated—with height was it? People on them became drugged into temporary well-being, like on a beach. Tonight the clouds were whistling—he heard them. Gomorrah looked good from here. Walking up to the two girls, he felt sinuous, as if his underwear had changed to silver.

"Be twins," he said, the backs of his hands prickling. "Then I can choose blind."

"We thought you'd never get here," the brown one said. "I'm Dina, this is Maureen. Have some champagne, it's free."

"She thinks you're crashing." The blond one smiled at him.

"Don't you?"

"She thinks you work here," the brown one said.

"Don't you?" Maureen asked.

"Not yet."

"Or maybe you're with Claes?" Dina said it slyly.

"Not yet."

"We are." Maureen was the straightforward one—it was just the hair.

"Maureen is—she works for Art Galaxy; I just hung along."

"We heard there was going to be a buffet."

102

"A hot one." Dina said.

"Oh, there will be. Hot meatballs. Hot shrimp." He tried to see the place in their light. About his age, but not like the girls he'd known here. Not school-types. High school, and then jobs, it would be. Job jobs, with no auras to them. No teaching in the most unique nursery school in Cambridge, like Monica Ellsworth—hah, he'd remembered her name. Applecheeks. The speed freak.

"You crash regular?" Dina.

"I j-just got back today." He didn't want to own up to this place.

"I told you, Maureen. Din' I? He has that overseas look." Dina stared moodily into the wheel of hors d'oeuvre in front of the impassive barman. Scooped up two. "My boyfriend, he's been back since months."

Ever since she lost her job, they'd been eating by following the crash lists. "You look in the papers for club activities; you call the magazines. Sometimes the designers' shows, even." The freeload list was endless. "Gee, isn't New York wonderful?"

Where was she from? She scooped up a salmon-round and a deviled egg. "How anybody can like caviar. Hmm? Oh—Lindenhurst."

Maureen came from the Bronx. "We live in a project. A good one though." Parkchester. Her folks' name was Breitwieser. "Wish Arnie could see this place." Her intended. She was working at Galaxy because Arnie

103

wanted to be in art. Right now he was working as a baker for her father. Her mother did hand-knits for the big stores.

"Her mother knits all her clothes. Naturally." Dina lowered her lids at him. There was a spark there.

"What a fab place. I wish Arnie. Who lives here?" They both looked at him expectantly.

"Ordinary people." He felt frightened. It was true. And he might be ashamed of it.

"Come on, must be some tycoon—look at the appetizers." Dina patted a last one down. "Now I'll wait for the buffet." Her friend was meeting her here. Then they'd all four go out to Maureen's. She and the friend had met Maureen at a guru lecture Saturday, in Town Hall. " 'Nourishment,' the ad said. But it turned out to be spiritual."

"You into yoga, Maureen?" He was surprised.

"My study group went. It's very popular." Her soft, almost r-less accent ran the words together. Ve-wee. He would take it from her tongue like a caramel. Would her intended? She saw him looking at her tiny diamond ring. "See those engraved places, alongside? That's for where you can add to it. As you work up."

"What'll you add?"

"Baguettes." The word wet her lip like a rainbow.

"Excuse me," she said, "but do you know where the bathroom is?"

He didn't, down here. "Let's ask him."

"Back of the kitchen, there's one," the butler said.

Hired for the day. He looked like an old prizefighter. Tight in the blazer, worn. What was it like to stand by, not listening? The man took Maureen's champagne glass as she went.

"Get off the ice." The girl Dina, at his elbow, whispering it.

"What do you mean?"

"What I said. This is our trick, Fred's and mine. She's going to ask us home. For the night."

As the two women he'd spoken to before ambled to the drink table, holding out their glasses, Dina turned her back to them, facing him, dug a steel finger in his rib, swept a small salver's contents into her pouch, already open, then took a second look at the little tray, pinched that too, and stared up at him like a sprung cat.

He'd never seen it done before. Common occurrence. Way his knife must have gone. Made the party seem closer. "Thought Freddie was coming here."

"Fred, to you. No, he won't make the rounds. Only in the park. I'll call him where he waits, tell him to meet us there. He's like—you know—still in ambush . . . You came out pretty good, didn't you?"

The party was more crowded now, people coming in through doors of rooms still unknown to him. Anybody in ambush, would have to be careful here. He couldn't see his parents anywhere. Buddy was always hard to find in a crowd. From here, the terrarium couldn't be seen. "How'd you know I was in?"

She shrugged. "Dime a dozen. Wait and see. You got a place?"

He nodded.

"Don't crowd us then, see. Maybe you can turn a trick here."

"Maybe." Now that she was closer, he smelled the cold, leathery odor of people who bedded outside or anywhere, of himself two nights ago. He could only smell it because he was here. "Does Freddie—Fred—trick in the park?"

"Trade, you mean? You wouldn't say that, he was here. He'd knock you off." Suddenly she perked her tam; the two women were passing. "He makes his own kind of rounds," she said airily. "You thinking of it? You don't look right for it. You don't know how, you might knock somebody off for good." She shivered. The steel finger went in his ribs again. Her trick, maybe. "Lay off then, huh?"

People thronged around them. "What are you going to do? At the Breitweisers?"

"Take a bath. Sleep. Be in a house." She crossed her arms and clutched her shoulders. "If I can get him in a house. We got kicked out of my residence club. I snuck him in. Oh, all the girls do it; these days a management winks. But Fred . . . sometimes he's still pretty animal. They threw us out." She looked up at Bunty. "Not sex, you know. No, no, no—if you want the sad truth. But hotels are no good to him, even flophouses. He always makes for the park. To jobhunt from there, it's hard. And I dunno, nine to five gets harder, the longer you don't. So I figure, get him in a house. Get that organized." She bent, cleaning the nail of her mid-finger with that hand's thumb. "Felipe could cook up a storm, once. Felipe's Fred. Maybe that intended of hers will get him a union card. She says bakers aren't the same as foodhandlers but she'll try." She smiled suddenly, walked over the table, took up a loaded tray and held it out to him. "So lay off."

"Guess you couldn't go back to Lindenhurst." A statement of kinship. Nobody he knew could.

"You kidding? I knew a German girl from there, once."

He saw how green he was.

"Fred and me both come from the Coast, we worked a spa there. I did. Oh on the up-and-up, in the sauna, a receptionist even. I got him on as a poolcleaner. An elegant joint. Only when the customers saw me with a Chicano, my share of the tips stopped. So Felipe and I worked our way east."

His eyes unfocused, over the devotion of women. And on Maureen, wending her way back to them. A man stopped her, in the cocktail way. She was bantering with him. But even from here it was plain she still had her eye on the baguettes. Buxom in her woolly, she looked like a nice pink house.

"Listen Dina," he said hurriedly. "I've got a wad—made hay in a crapgame last night. Here, take some; don't go out there." He peeled off two hundred left from what Buddy had last sent him. "To the Bronx, I mean."

"Jesus." She held it in front of her.

"Put it away." Across the floor, Buddy was waving at him, pushing gently through the crowd. Maureen, going toward the library now for some reason, must in a moment bump into him. And the two of them—into Dina and him. Lines of force. There must be about sixty people at his birthday party; with luck, he would hear the life-story of only two.

"Why you giving it to me for? You got the hots for Maureen, huh?"

"I've already got a girl."

"I'll bet."

"Why latch onto her, that's all. She's her kind of nice girl, that's all. And you know what her folks would be."

Dina raised her eyelashes. "Like mine. Just because you saw me pinch the dinky tray, huh." The money was still in her hand. "Here."

"No, take it anyway."

"You want me to scram, huh. How?"

"You could go to the bathroom. And not come back."

"And leave her in a lurch? That's worse isn't it—than going out there?"

"Would it be?"

She wouldn't look at him.

"I'll send her home in cab."

"Oh. Like good girls get. And what's in it for you?"

What was? At the parties he was used to, rapping was the style—that's what the parties were for. Though being in style made it harder. "I don't know."

She smiled down at the money. "You just like Felipe. Impractical."

"Am I?" He started to be pleased.

"Get it from those Asians. That's what. Okay—Jesus, here comes somebody." She flipped open the pouch at her waist, thought better of it. Smiled like a movie-still.

"Dinner's being served," his father said. "In the dining car."

At parties Buddy still went blackface. Poor guy, a marked man. City College, circa 1945.

"We're enjoying your party, sir." He prayed his father would think this was the way he was with girls. "This is Dina."

She held out a graceful, empty hand. She must have stashed it. Had Buddy seen—in time?

"I'm—er, C-Carroll Monteith, sir." Bunty said. "We're just leaving." He gave his father what he hoped was the high sign. Of a man who had just made an arrangement. Yale School of Architecture, 1976.

"Pip-pip," Buddy said, raising his brows. "Good-oh. Quick journey, Mr., er—Monteith. Visit, I mean. Will we see you again? Later this evening perhaps." He turned on his heel, his shoulders angry.

"He knows we crashed," she said.

"Let's go," he said, sunk. "I'll go find Maureen. You go the other way."

"Bye."

He stopped short. It was always so final. "Bye."

But Maureen was nowhere to be found.

He circled back to the terrace, in case Maureen had. Dina was still there. He saw she knew.

She took his arm. "She left a pink stole in that room over there, when we came in. Let's go check."

There wasn't much there to paw among—gloves, jackets, one umbrella, a few scarves. It was still summer.

"No, she scrammed. Guess I told her too much." Dina swung around nonchalantly, scanning. "Guess this is the library. No books. But it always is." She was shivering.

"Want me to get you a wrap?"

She laughed. "Where?"

"I'll find something." Maeve left furniture behind like successive skins, but saved everything she had ever worn. Like skin.

"That your racket? No thanks. When the leaves turn, maybe. Then maybe I'll come back for mink." She did a time-step. "Gee, a song . . . Don't think we haven't thought of it."

"Haven't got a racket. Yet."

"Well, don't start one here, the barman's onto us. He said he'd seen me before. I think he's a Pinkerton."

"What's that?"

"Where'd you grow up? They hire them. To watch." She came up to him, tugged his jacket. "I *was* going to scram. All by myself. Couldn't you see that? Want your money back?"

"Is Freddie real? Fred I mean. Felipe."

It took her a while. "He has a bad sphincter muscle. And a citation. But they still throw him out for it. He soils sheets. And her mother hand-knits them, probably."

"Do you really sleep in the park?"

"Not always. Last night we did. Near the chess place. It depends. Sometimes I can get him to check in somewhere. If he has a stake. Sometimes somebody asks us in."

In the corner there was a flowered sink, with a wastebasket underneath. He watched her empty the leather pouch, daintily clean it out, fill the washbowl again and sink into it to her upper arms. The soap was perfumed. She inhaled deeply. "Luxury is everywhere."

It was always one of the good times out, seeing a pretty woman wash. There would always be a little more to this one's story than she said. Or a little less. It was attractive, the way laziness was. And crummy bars. And runt dogs.

"No, please keep the money. But I'd love to know where you stashed it. I couldn't figure out."

She picked up her tam by its button and held it aloft. The money wafted slowly past her grave face, and down.

For some reason, that killed him. Her too. A feeling that felt it could shed itself, pressed them together.

Not misery but the excitement that came of it, more from her, but some from him. Under her dress she

Eagle Eye

had nothing on—when he looked surprised, she murmured, "Threw them away this morning. They threw themselves away. My pants." As he closed with her, he murmured back, "No, I'm just always surprised it's the same shape." They crushed briefly together. He should have locked the door first, but no one came in anyway. What he'd meant about shape was that women who came on like a pack of assorted . . . cared—deuces and treys, eights and aces—ought to show it down there somehow. What did it matter. Almost at once he was able to offer his handkerchief to tuck between her legs. She did that. Locked against his chest, she listened to what couldn't get out of there, the heart he wanted to be proud of. Holding her head, he heard the tears that couldn't fall. This was the kind of girl he always got.

She was at the sink again when she said, "I wanted to be in a house, that's all."

"I was overseas. But not with the war."

When they left the room she had the silver salver in her hand; she had polished it. "I'll leave it with the Pinkerton." He waited for her at the housedoor, in front of the Nevelson. She came back, dreamily. "He wasn't there. But he'll know. He saw me take it. Anyway, I won't be coming back here."

"Wait."

He ran back through the house and up the stairs. The bedrooms were new to him, but much the same. In the one that must be Maeve's, he went straight to the double armoire where her coats would be. There they were, in a sequence like a memory, all the way back to the department stores. He chose one from somewhere before the middle of them—brown and thick, not seen for a long time. Then switched it for a prettier one, with fur. Down the back way, he met no one.

She was still standing there. Something she must have done to herself while he was away had made her look to him as she had in the beginning. Women never looked too bad when they were waiting like that. She didn't move when he draped the coat on her.

"For winter."

Locking her thumbs in the coat's lapels, she hung on. She knew when not to say anything. Did she suspect he didn't have to leave? What did she think of him, more or less?

Downstairs, under the canopy, she bent back, gazing up at it. White, with three twined initials in gold braid. Like a monogrammed sheet. "Get *me* a cab?"

He ran for one. Fifth Avenue had none; he picked up one on Madison, rode it back and jumped out just in time. She was just walking away, head down. Toward the park.

"You have to expect more," he said, grabbing her. She let him tuck her in. When he gave the driver some bills, she glowed.

"He wants to know where." She could go to a hotel. But of course she knew that.

Leaning forward, she told the driver to go down Columbus Avenue. "Eighty-third or fourth, maybe." A bar called the Lotos, on the west side of the street. "No, maybe seventy-third. I'll show him where." Freddie Felipe could trust her still. Her shrug was merry. "Our bathroom and kitchen facilities. We walk to it."

He reached through the window to squeeze her hand. "Check you at the Lotos, sometime."

"What are you, a talent scout?"

As the cab pulled away, though, she leaned out and gave him the sign he'd gone around the world with. Be with it. Right on. Peace. Whatever you took it to be. He'd made her happy then, or generous. He took it that he still could be proud of his heart.

Upstairs again, waiting for someone to come and deal with the three locks that told who the Bronsteins were, he still smiled, for the generalized love that only the ones who were his age, stamping forward and along the old lottery paths, knew how to take.

Whoever had come to the door was having trouble.

For the moment while the locks clicked; number one—human manual, number two—electronic Siamese, number three—a soft slatching, like the roller-bearings at Dachau, he ducked into one of his mowzels and was back with his own kind. Damphaired fur, close rawhide, thong and toe, calico smoke. Wherever the drum thumps, the poetry machines are grinding for the night. The swish of the snares, seineing the bottoms for no meaning, is always a beach sound. What-ho the bonny crevices of all the wars you're not going to. Heave-to, to the bonny advices of all the girls who are not ashamed of it. Lie down with us, in the drag-wail of the dixie cups. Onka-bonka, what a boss drummer. Going to the front, onka-bonka. Right here.

His father opened the door to him. " 'Bout time. She's got a birthday cake." Down the years, he and Bunt had disavowed the sentiment of it, two boys together under Maeve's silly yoke.

As Buddy shunted them down the necessary halls to the dining room, he swung a locker-room arm up and over Bunt's shoulder. "Don't want to butt in, you and girls, Bunt. Far from. But at your age, I sure hate to see money have to change hands."

They had stopped dead anyway. He slipped Buddy's arm off. Size had never been a sorrow between them. But it was time his father dealt with all six-and-a-half feet of him. "Be a Montefiore, Buddy? Not a Rothschild?"

Sure, he had hit him. Maybe it was time to say anything. Without being depressed.

The dining room, full up now, was a shock. All those faces, hanging over the pink-linen trough the main table had been made into, bobbling at him monkey-eyed, ass-chinned, kitty-smooching, diminishing down the room in one of those longshots cameramen took kneeling, out of some nice A-rated movie that had broken its guarantee not to turn into a dream. The sad fact was, it took youth not to look like some other animal than our brand. They all looked like they knew their own ravages. And were counting on a good boy like him to be the kinder for it. They were still in the saddle—and he had better watch it; they wanted to take him along. Oh, he knew where he was, all right. Maybe the women weren't decked out like the Brooklyn of those days, but he knew the smell of those salted almonds. The wine in these glasses might be a little better, and technically this wasn't a hall—but after all, he was older than the usual candidate.

Just then, Doughty pranced in and up to him. A Harlequin Dane wasn't his style, up to now not the Bronsteins' either, but a dog is a dog. An animal that is an animal. He fed him a couple of almonds, making the picture they were planned to. "Doughty," he said to the cocked ear, "bet you never been to a bar mitzvah before."

He'd been seated at the big table's far end, his parents at the other. Looking down the line, he saw that Maeve's "do" hadn't changed much—the people maybe, but not their categories. Leskel, the man on his left, was the one who had asked to meet Buddy, at his own graduation. The lady on his right, a nice camel with big droopy eyes, said, "We're in your parents' box." The opera. On her right was a big tawny-haired man Leskel introduced as Dr. Somebody. The hair long for these parts. Or for him. On Leskel's left, the gal who had admired the rug informed him she was from Maeve's class at the Alliance Française. His parents hadn't thank God placed him between the two of them. There were no place cards. "Just sprinkle," was what Maeve would have said, or Buddy. There wasn't that much time, to know who your friends were.

Maeve was still here. He kept an eye on her.

"The best gilt glasses, Buddy. I see you kept those." His father was pouring him wine. The glasses were from the last place, and really something. They'd never drunk from them before.

"When it gets to be art, you can keep it on," his father said. "All the years it took to find that out. Something is gone though. Thought you'd notice right out."

"Never thought you noticed I noticed . . . It would've looked like fool, with that harpsichord."

"Would it? Anyway, I saved it. You'll see. That little Kranich & Bach has integrity." Buddy winked.

He winked back. Like he knew his father was a tried man. "Okay, saved by a piano." He put a hand on Buddy's shoulder, locker-room style. "Okay, we're still in love."

Leskel was envying them. His hair still had a round cut; the trim bags under his eyes were impressionist. "You know my boy Johnny? He's living with a girl."

That's Johnny-boy. "Not to worry." Bunt said. "They all come from very good families."

"Oh, I know." Leskel brightened. "The mother and father came to look us over. To plead us to do something. When they saw how we lived—they calmed down. We even had a foursome of bridge. Best partners Dollie and I ever had."

"Maybe they'll make it legal someday."

"Think there's a chance?"

"The foursome? Oh–the best." He leaned forward; a glint had caught his eye. But the tawny man had turned his back.

Mrs. Camel was waiting for Bunt's regard. "I saw the way you looked at us. Can't blame you. But wait 'til it's your turn." She had a smiling competence he recognized, but couldn't place. Direct, and hopeful-hopeless.

"Oh, I won't mind so much getting old. If I can get my life right. But I'll hate it for the girls I know."

"Oh, they'll manage." When she laughed, the eyes lifted. The red hair looked real as his own. "You just stop being a girl."

He saw Maeve slip out again.

"You look a little like a girl I knew." Monica's eyes went that way, already. "But with her anything can happen. She's a speed freak."

"Oh, so are mine. All six of them. The situation around our house is terrible. Eight cars of course. But then, four Hondas and a hovercraft. Plus the two planes."

Some mothers—that's what he'd recognized. Where there were a lot of kids, like once. She could hang on, or let go; whether or not she knew the score, she was the center of it. At graduation there had been some like her. "You married? I mean—" He blushed.

She exploded.

So did he. "I mean you're not a widow or anything."

"My husband flew us in. I expect he's in Honduras by now."

"Airline pilot?"

She smiled a no.

"Revolutionary?"

"You are a romantic, aren't you."

"No, a wit. I mean, who else would have six kids. Except maybe the Kennedys."

"He owns the airline."

"Oh, that's right. Silly of me." The opera box. They were rich enough to have six kids, not poor enough to. And Maeve's pick-up's husbands so often had business elsewhere.

"You Catholic?" he said. It was on his mind, that he might give in.

"My husband is. And the children, of course."

"You women. You can do anything."

"*You women*. Where did you pick that up?"

He looked her over. Yes, she looks like Paulina, like—like any of them, when you get down to it. Like all of them, at that certain moment when. If he said—Let's go somewhere, you and me; let's get out of here; see here, I have this awful hangnail I need help about; or even, you're pretty vulnerable, you need to talk; or any of the one-hundred-ninety-seven unconsecrated versions of it—more variations than his knife had, and more reliable—she'd give in. Maybe she didn't know that yet; maybe she thought he didn't. Asking is the flattery. More than anything. He wouldn't though.

119

Eagle Eye

No one over thirty, so far. So far, no one over twenty-six, which is what Jasmin is. Keep the bloodlines clear.

"I'm scared I'll be too adjustable, that's all. It's the one thing scares me blue."

"Your principles, you mean?" She was already over the romantic hump, examining her rings with a tycoon-ess cool that made him think less of her. You could commit hara-kiri on anyone of them. But she had asked.

"I'm only romantic about what I want. Or I will be. Not over the rest of it."

She closed her eyes and said something to herself. *Jesus*, he thought it was. Appropriate, for a convert.

On her right, the big fellow Leskel had introduced as Doctor, leaned forward. "I hear you say you want to live right?"

"Listen, I was only trying to say anything. Anything I really thought. It was an experiment."

"How'd it work out?"

Bunty looked him over closer. In profile, the man's hedge of hair really vibrated up, like an electric shoe-brusher with a kind forehead. Or a man on the hotseat, smiling all the same.

"Too easy, if you want to know. When a place is not your style, anyway. And it doesn't get you anywhere."

"You don't like it here?" she interrupted. "The son of the house?" South American curves on top she had, and under the table what he'd bet would be long country-club stems. He had a suspicion that, closer to forty, which

120

she must be, the attraction was that the parts didn't match. But what he wanted to see was that doctor's ear.

"Everybody has his own way of dwarfing the world," he said, low. "This just isn't mine."

"Where *do* you want to go?" The doctor's voice.

Back to where it hurts, is Jasmin's idea. She said she intends to spend the rest of her life there.

He raised his eyes. "You our new family doctor?"

"Partly." He had a way of listening in profile, eyes cocked sideways. Like a teaching nun. Or a monk. Or one of the children at their skirts.

Right on. "You're Buddy's shrink."

He winced. And there it was, the thin gold wire in the bush of his sideburn. Like one more gold hair, thickened with listening. There couldn't be two of them with that in an ear.

Should he ask, or leave it be. Choose.

"You're Janacek, aren't you? The child psychologist?"

He bowed. "And you are Bunt."

Who floats in Buddy's mind, like a hovercraft? "How'd you come to know—us?"

Leskel spoke. "Through us."

He was stunned at the way it could work out. And encouraged. Chance can happen. Good or bad, you have to cherish it. "Aren't you a child psychiatrist?"

Another bow. "Sometimes the children are—grown. You know my work?"

121

Eagle Eye

"I—knew one of them."

Janacek smiled, but didn't ask who. Probably gets it all the time; there are so many of them. Besides the one he's married to.

It didn't take a minute, to dovetail her story with this bowing man's. And feel for both of them. "A dirty story he had nothing to do with," she said. "Ten years old at Buchenwald, Bunt—Long Island is full of them. And Washington Heights." But his mother had been a camp guard. And was still alive. Until recently. He wore the wire, Jasmin said, for kids to focus on. And it's true, Bunt—you look at it, in that hair, and you're back in fairyland where the grass has eyes, and there's a gold ring in the pond. "He has very strong lines of force," she said, "but he doesn't hurt enough, anymore."

He was exerting them. "Like to talk to you, Bronstein. About your parents. And you of course."

K-k-k, Bronstein. The story attracts *you*.

"S-sorry. Thanks though."

"Why not?"

Up at the head of the table, Buddy tapped a fork against a glass. It rang true, of course.

"There's my majority coming up. Let's leave it at that."

"You could help so."

"I plan to."

"Why not let me help you to?"

"Hold it, Kid Bronstein," Buddy had seen Maeve was gone. "A slight delay. Practice your speech."

He saluted. *"Coming, Father!"* Buddy and Ike's favorite comic, the early days. A comic son.

"You're a very interesting young man. You could help *me*."

He puts his empathy right in your hand, Jasmin says. He has to have you have it. That's why she left; that's why she goes back. It's the secret of his success with the kids, she said. He's non-rejectable.

He could try. "Thanks. But I don't think you're the teddy bear I always wanted."

He looks puzzled. Human flesh shows no prints. At least, mine doesn't yet. And maybe she never went back to him. But the echoes of people in one another last on and on.

As is my hope.

"We—have met?" Echoes were the man's trade, after all.

He could pass it up. Chance strolled by him, a gainly dog; he gave it his hand to bite. "Yes, we have, Dr. Jannie. In a launderette. You came by with Jasmin's check."

Janacek knew her habits, she said, and couldn't give the habit up. In bed after, in the room paid for by the check perhaps, he'd felt uneasy, but she'd said not to; she didn't need the money, really. Let Jannie think he was protecting her. She let him come back some-times—yes, into bed even—because she was the only one with whom he could be a child. They'd agreed not to have them because of his work. And her views. "It's

a rotten sell for kids these days. I shan't have one."
She'd agreed to have Jannie though, not knowing. "You
can't desert a child," she said, laughing, and tugged at
his own red hair. "Kangaroo-oo."

To his right, Mrs. Camel, mother of six, was now
talking seriously with Leskel, who had moved around
to her. They look so grown, most of them, no matter
what's inside. Opposite him, Janacek's earring glinted,
joining him to childhood. Perhaps one day, Bronstein
himself would find himself wanting one.

Janacek was staring at him. "Yes, she spoke of you.
Many times. Ah, yes."

"How is Jasmin these days? I should call her up."

Sorry—I'm always rude when I have to wear a tie.

"How long have you been away, Bronstein?"

"Nine months. Wrote her from Paris." After
Monica? No, before. "But she never wrote back."

"Poor boy." Janacek grasped him by the jacket. "Sit
down."

His father was chiming at his glass again. The table
straightened and took up the chime, old dinosaurs
chocking their bow ties sideways at the guest of honor—a
dowager iguana, a donkey with the usual whimsical
specs.

Cows were harder to come by. In a pinch might
two priests do? One black, one white.

"Can't now. What's up?"

Janacek sat down. Slowly.

It came to him then. What it must be. Of course.

Underneath the din, he said it aloud. "She's pregnant. That it? And it's mine."

For five seconds, hilarity had me. Report that as my reaction to fatherhood. Not everybody can find that out beforehand. At his own bar mitzvah. And as a candidate for the Catholic Church.

In retrospect it seems a long time. Farce would have been so lovely. Of God.

Janacek bent forward across the table, pulling me toward him. Five seconds more were awarded me. In which I called Jasmin up. His earring brushed me then. I recoiled. His eye had passed me on the way, an old red searchlight.

"She fell in Bryant Park, an anti-war day crowd. The autopsy showed a very light skull."

The glasses went on chiming true.

"To our son on his twenty-first," my father said. Maeve had come back. He raised his glass to me. The first time I'd seen him so, he'd been in his first custom-made tux, toasting himself in a mirror as the best dressed goddam penguin he ever saw—and I'd bawled with an eight-year-old's rage because it was so true-not-true. "To my son. Not a prodigal. But returned."

Eagle Eye

Buddy is a graceful man.
Grace, past or present, breaks me up.

Program me in now, Betts.
Betts?

There was a disappointed murmur at the conclusion
of my speech, a one-liner I remembered from what a
boy says on that day. Murmur more approving as the
word went round that I had achieved tears. Buddy
saluted me. Maeve put out a hand like a ghost feeling.
I sat down.

"Maybe you'll come talk to me now?" Dr. Jannie
said. The children called him that; sometimes she did.
She talked about him more after I'd seen him; that was
natural. Still, there are these people you never expect
to have to deal with personally. Even if you know their
sadness perfectly, maybe even seeing their story, seeing
around it, just a little different from the person telling
you it. Even so—he had been only a character in my
friend's life.

But just now, I had had my first real death. And
I noticed something about it that people never tell you.
Not even the poets, who are supposed to have the high
sign on it. From now on, Jasmin was going to be only
a character in living peoples lives. She was only going
to be something that had happened to *us*. Oh, we could
tell each other stories. About what had happened
between her and us. We could explore it forever. But

nothing could ever change for her. On her own. She had no more chance.

"M-maybe I will." I didn't know whether I could bear to help the process along.

But that was for later. I knew what had happened to me, too.

I looked down the table. Oh yes oh yes, I was pretty young for what had happened to me; for a long while yet, it mightn't show. But I had joined the animals. A voice was telling me so. A character in my life. "*Kangaroo*," it said to me. *Kangeroo-oo*.

Maeve was looking down the long, buzzing table, at Jannie and me. No, at him. At least lift a glass to me, Maeve, throw me a kiss, even a department-store kiss. After all, it's my twenty-first. Her glass stood primly unused; I hadn't watched. At the time of the toast, I was elsewhere in time. Only a few minutes ago. But I remembered a time for Maeve and me when she couldn't take her eyes off me. From about my eighth to eleventh year, it was the worst. Or when I got conscious of it. I'd raise my eyes from my oatmeal or math book; or even while I was talking; I'd bump into hers. "Stop *looking* at me." She'd shake her head, shake her glance away, and only smile. Ten minutes later, I'd catch her back at it. "I love the shape of your head, that's all," she said once. "I just like to look at it." And reached out and smoothed my hair. When I got too tall for her to do that without stretching, she stopped. About the time of Paulina, my first girl, of course. But I couldn't buy that, much. Or that when it came due to toast me, Maeve felt vibes from Jasmin.

It was the other way round. Jasmin was making me feel Maeve's. Of all the girls since Paulina, all those who hung in my mind like upside-down pretty torsos——not bloody at all, white as candy, tan as sand, all swaying in the wind like a gentle town on wasyday that I whizz by on my motorbike—Jasmin is now the one who's right-side up, a speaking girl. She has a good head on her shoulders now. Thinskulled as it is, it can talk to me. She's permanent.

She's telling me what I always knew, even at eight. That Maeve, next to Buddy, with him, was always one person, Maeve alone another. What I see now though, is something new.

"That's your mother, isn't it?" Janacek says. "I've not met her yet. That's why I came. But I haven't managed to. You know she won't talk to any of us?"

"Why should she?"

"Only that sometimes this means the person has a very bad thing inside, that dare not be said."

A child's vocabulary. But it ticks.

Maeve is sitting beside Buddy; they're together. But Maeve is now Maeve alone. That's the difference. Is that so bad it can't be said?

I see now that she's not looking at either of us. Not at the doctor, not at me. There are still vibrations between her and me, from a lifetime together, but she's unaware I'm catching them. That is another difference.

What if she's not keeping things anymore? Objects.

People. Not keeping them even to change them, to throw them out for something else. Not even keeping the coats —to be kept. And if she's not keeping Buddy, the vibes tell me, is it a matter of divorce?

You don't divorce a child, a son. An only son and child. And my majority has nothing to do with it. If her gaze travels past me, it has nothing to do with sons-and-mothers jazz, or any of the psycho-dramas well-meaning people are told of. She's not keeping me on—that's clear. Clear from the moment I entered the house, if I'd looked at it. Sure it hurts. But is that the worst?

"But she did invite you here," I said to Janacek.

"I doubt she even knows my name. Your father did. He invited us all."

"*He* did. How do you know?"

"He talks to me now and then you know."

"I see."

Standard for what people say when they don't, Betts. An adult phrase. Hilarity even came over me again; maybe that's what chance is.

Remember Tufts, our programming in-structor, came to the school twice a week from down in Dutchess County, where lives the IBM God he was always going to take us on a day-trip to see; but did never? How he used to tweak the ears of those he liked best, the ones who were serious—usually you and me—just when we had our heads bent, going at it hardest, how that jarring tug would come, in an arc that made us see stars. Treats us like reform-school boys, I said to you; what if he is such a good man at his stuff? You said no, studying was like a surface-tension you could get glued in; he wanted us to kick past. He ruined a set-up for me once though. But when he came to you, you'd already put everything to bed lightning fast and were ready for him. He bent down sideways, like a great wheedling moon, and said, "Right, Betts. You can tug *my* ear." Though you were our best, we marveled. "How you handled him!" we all said. "Sweet drunk, like my father, I know what to expect." You said to me later. Oh, you were our best. Not why I chose you though, to help me out here.

Remember how I visited you in India? Just four months ago, in the small house that fitted you too well. With its over-large nameplate. Never knew your middle name was Maitland. Fits you fine. I had never visited such a house before. You could tell me nothing, of all I knew you knew. Somehow I had to make you talk to me of those feverish school-days—the lab hours after which you and I crept back to work and came out dazzled, walking across the yard in a silent double-migraine, to slide just in time into our seats in mess-hall, to chomp cold broccoli, cornbeef and ice cream—while the universal chessmen marched in our heads. With Tufts' astral voice still barking at us what we called "Tufts' Lord's prayer." *Reorganize the problem*; define it.

Determine the method; mechanize the method. Break down the chart. Remember human error. Debug. The flow-diagram is the flow of logic. Code from the diagram. *Test* . . . Getting the application into production never really interested him; he was a teaching man; how we respected him for that! . . . But about that day at dinner—standing near you in the heavy Indian sun, I reminded you of it, and of what you had done. We were a school that said grace before a meal and gave thanks again after, very Protestant, each boy taking his turn; that day it was yours. You'd always laughed at me for loving the computer terminology for its old associations; the "assertion box"—by using which, Tufts said, a processor could assert his own individuality; the "memory box"—where the installation stores. These terms were chosen like the Oedipus complex they talked about in psych class, you said. "Just a throwback to a former world." And I said, *"I'm a throwback."*

But that day, when you stood up to say grace, you winked at me. *Enable all traps!* you barked, and the hall roared. When you stood up again at meal's end, they were snuffling expectantly through their winter-wet noses. Real computer language was what you loved, those agreed-upon alphabets that couldn't be profaned—the very name ALGOL could wake your smile. You stood up, fiddled stagily with the remains on your plate, wrinkled your high Northumberland nose. All drunks have drama in them, you once said. *Remember human error*, you said, and walked out. When the headmaster called you in afterwards, you were lectured not on your manners to God, but on the difficulty of keeping publicly insulted cooks. "So much for the application of knowledge, Bunty," you said.

So when you turned eighteen, Tufts got you a research job at IBM. I visited you there too, the last time I saw you, except one. You had your own installation, or the squire's share of it. "Still call it Batface?" I said, but got no answer; you were over my head now. And maybe IBM's. They had you working on sub-routines, for godsake. But you were twenty, not in college, and war-vulnerable. On a nearby memo pad, somebody had written: Define Macro Skeleton. "What's MACRO?" I said. "I forget?" I saw you were dashed. "A form of pseudo-instruction." But it came back to me like a long ride on the motorbike, after months of nothing between the knees but women. "Or vice versa," you said. By after dinner, we had each covered our respective miles. On your desk there was a book called *Calculating Engines*. "Charles Babbidge, born 1792. Anticipated everything. Including IBM's new 7090." I asked what that was. "This." You laid a hand on it, like a man does on the throbbing that owns him. "Batface."

Then looked at me darkly, lively fairhaired Anglo as you still were, silver under night's study-lamp. "Don't you fall for any of Norbert Wiener's leftover boys, Bunty pal. Predicting the black future when computers get out of control. All the future's already in the past, see. And ready for us. *All of it.*"

I reminded you I wasn't at Harvard, but merely at a nearby institution, where I had taken pains to see that my most complicated course was one on Whitehead and Russell. "In words, John. That old terminology. I've wonked out on the other. It's too applicable, just now. And MIT is dirty well applying it."

I was eighteen now, and my draft number was low. We discussed ways of not going. "Ways of not applying ourselves," you said. "You'll go on playing it by ear, Bronstein, I know you." You were going out to New Delhi. For a subsidiary of IBM.

"Where the needs are still very binary," you said, with your old smile.

This I remembered. "Tuft's law." It was Tuft's contention that since computers talk in binary code—based on the number 2, instead of the decimal—and since man, from feet to hands all the way to the on-off nerve systems of the brain was himself such a collection of twosomes, that the computer was therefore as human as any of his creations to date. Sometimes Tufts would use "binary" and human interchangeably; one Christmas he gave us a discourse on "binary" love.

"Where's he now?"

I hadn't known he was dead. Of the error of drink.

The Lord is dead, I thought, but I can smell his disciple, in the early Fishkill morn. On my way out, you made me a present of Babbidge. I have to say I never read him fully; backpacking is hard on the mind. But when I found you in New Delhi, not at the address on your card, but no trouble at all, I remembered what you'd said of him as I left. "The government gave him seventeen-thousand pounds to build his Analytical Engine. He couldn't, because the mechanical skills of the age weren't equal to the job. He once said he'd swap the rest of his life for three days, five-hundred years later. And look." You jerked a finger at Batface. "Less than a hundred and fifty years, Bunt. Isn't that sad?"

I thought of that when I saw you again. John Maitland Betts, you were right. All your future was in the past. You knew what to expect.

I seem to be collecting sadnesses. A backpack is more expansible than I thought. Don't mention skeletons to me, Betts, for a while. But that day, looking down at you in your house-grave, I thought I could define yours. There's a country beetle that winds its horn out there around four o'clock, maybe to remind one to listen to the heat's silences and be warned; you didn't seem to hear. Your head will never again be your house.

I trust you to hear me now. The mechanical means now provided being my own memory-box. With those synapses they say spurt each to each, in an input-output of two by two. Help me recognize the problem. I'll determine the method. *Ignore all traps* or interruptions due to time, distance and graves. In the termination of Batfaces anywhere, we shall *disable* them.

Hear old Tufts' voice, homing like a four-o'clock beetle in the after-hours of prep-school America. "But, disciples, the computer remembers any disabled traps. And when they are finally *en-abled*, as we say it, they take place in a built-in sequence. Oh beautiful, gentlemen. Socko beautiful."

Then came the swig from the vest-pocket flask, brought out with a stiff one-two-three flexion: fingers, elbow, mouth—a ritual that he honored for a priestly moment afterward, eyes closed. Then went on talking, as if it had all been done in the dark. "And disciples, the building of systems which are to operate in real environments—with people! With other machines! With nature!—that's the real challenge in programming."

We found it all in our manual, later. But it remained as he said, beautiful. *Enable all traps.* Let the dining hall laugh. You and I could never get over the thrill of it. Of that sluice-gate moment when all the interruptions are cancelled, and the sequence pays off, pays and pays. How we squawked of it

Eagle Eye

to each other, from bicycle to bicycle, under the
Babbidge-light the stars were already sending us
from their past, while we rode through people,
machines and nature—all waiting to be hemmed
in. I thought I'd found a religion. At fifteen. You'd
found Tufts.
    I got over it.
    Because all computers have to be lied to, Betts.
At times. The data has to fit the problem. No moral-
ity involved. Old Batface will do exactly what you
tell it to—right or wrong. As all the manuals assure
us, it is the perfect fool.
    But it can't lie, like a man does. To itself.

    Recognize the problem, Betts? And right
behind you, Tufts? You two would make a good
audience. Best information processors a boy ever
had. The internal world of the 7090, deals in micro-
seconds; wouldn't any life be quickly dealt with?
But you could handle it alone, Betts, even from
the India of your little house.
    This particular installation—on whose magne-
tic tapes we could record all the data a twenty-
one-year-old life can muster—belongs to my father.
That won't matter. It doesn't know.
    Pick up your past, Bronstein. According to lead-
ing authorities, it has your future in it.
    Process the question. Start with any one of
them.

Why did Buddy lie?

Has he before? . . . . Put that in too . . . . And to whom.

EOF END OF FILE.

"I see," he said.

He saw Maeve was going to leave them again. In a minute she'll rise like a sleepwalker, pay them all her absent smile, and ease out that door, a plain refectory one, but thick as money could make 'em, when the year nineteen-hundred-and-twenty was bringing over monasteries from Spain.

J. P. Morgan and Hearst brought them, and the good Jewish bankers, working in their own way for Christ. Then the gangsters got them, and the theatre people. And now us. Underneath, are the monks and angels walking in the wood all the same, choralling from that tapestry up there, on whoever's wall? And those mini-animals that grin and glee down at the bottoms of Italian painting before perspective, heavy-headed little ghouls on pin-legs? Does Buddy know how much Europe has taught me? I can't see him as a monk, but I can in a Dutch burgher's hat, wide with finance. And in a ruff, the family one, stiff with grandfather-starch and lacy hints from the family women. Holding him up. He's staring out of the picture with the same pink abstraction about the eyes that Rembrandt saw clouding the eyes of one of the councilmen he painted; maybe they both had difficult wives at home. Since 1575, Dr. Jannie, that has been a worry. I can see why Buddy talks to you—even if neither of you knows.

When my father goes heavy and quiet like that, reddening like a solemn baby holding its breath against the bitter world, he never does anything physical. He's not even touching Maeve's hand. There was never anything to be scared of.

She's going to get up. Nevertheless.

I never saw my father before. Those lines of force.

Only—the door got there first. Opening with a rumble from the wheelchair behind. By now, every door in the house would have my grandmother's gouge in it. And every person she met. Maybe she had humor once; certainly there was sharpness; it's all gone to ill-will. Of the kind people our age simply don't have.

I don't mean to exalt us. It's only that in our own minds, we're still saving people, not discarding them. No matter what we *do*, we still have general connections, not specific ones. Not narrowed down. That's the barrier even between us and the next ones on—I've felt it already. I don't mind it being called innocence. I wish it could be kept. Sometimes, I almost think it can be. If I could teach memory not to chafe in one rut for so long that it finally has to justify that rut. I can try.

"Why, the woman's got an old AWVS uniform on." The lady on my right—Mrs. Camel. Mrs. Drexel Jackson, as she'd informed me. Now that I myself had joined the animals, I no longer saw her the other way.

"Mrs. Reeves, you mean? What uniform?"

"American Women's Voluntary Services, World War Two. That marvelous old blue."

Poor Reeves, hoping that when friends meet her along the Avenue, they'll think she's some kind of volunteer. But she needn't have; by now she's got that limp look of people whose story you pass by, you haven't got time for. I can tell she knows that's what her story is. At school, much as I hated to pass by people like that, I did. It's catching, otherwise.

Reeves brought the chair to a smart stop, waving her other hand meanwhile. She had our notice. Mother MacNeil helps her out there.

"Up on the balcony! Mother talked!"

My grandmother hadn't budged from what she was when I first saw her. Every morning, in Amenia, she combed her hair at the kitchen mirror with a liquid that kept it dark, yet scorned to do it secretly. Her hands hadn't spread with work, but gone pinched. In Leinster once, where her quarter of us had come from, on the border between Englishtown and Irishtown I met a postmistress reminded me of her. Wouldn't deign to read your mail, but begrudged you it. A Kilkenny cat. Jonathan Swift went to school there. And learned something.

None of us three family was eager to inquire what she'd said, up there on the balcony. Any miracle would be so strictly her own.

But Dr. Jannie leaned forward eagerly. "What did she say?"

"It was when Bunty answered his father's toast."
Reeves flushed, for the Yiddish maybe. If it was.

It was part of the gibberish the party-boy says at
one point to his father; I couldn't repeat it if I tried.
I had faked it. It was from where he seems to be saying
"A son. A son. A son is given." Or a man.

. . . 'A son is given' is from the Messiah, I know
that. We sang it in the glee club at the academy. And
'My son, my son'—that's David to Absalom. When he
finds him hanging. . .

But that's what I thought I said.

"She'd just been praying, as usual. She's saying the
Hail Mary, I think, if you listen close; I'm not too familiar
with it. Anyway, she says it eight times a day. Hail Mary
full of Grace. Either that, or else my name." Reeves
gave an odd smile. "Sometimes I think she confuses
the two of us. Anyway, she slammed the door of her
prayer-thing shut—she's got a lot of strength—and said
right out, "Hear that? They've got him. Get me
downstairs." Straight out. I had to bring her the back
way—where the ramp is. But now she's clammed up
again."

What *is* your name?"

Reeves eyes got bluer. Not only the uniform. Contact is hard to resist, even if manners tell you to. "Mary
Grace."

Mother MacNeil was struggling jealously. Her
mouth ran about like a mouse she couldn't catch.

Jannie gave her his full attention at once. "Yes yes,
yes yes *yes*." His hand smoothed hers, buttering it with

140

a new, light voice that came oddly out of his bear bulk. Yes, a dancing bear that somebody had long ago ringed. Neither an ugly cripple nor a handsome robot, yet his flat face, deep-slit eyes, and that long, plumb line from nose to upper lip, did make me think of toy-types like the Tin Woodsman or Pinocchio, some creature that had been created from behind, more plainly so than the rest of us. Not a ghoul, Jasmin had said, explaining why she had gone back to him—and why she left again. Only the ghoul's son. "With a mother like his, whom could one go to—to be a child?" She hadn't wanted to tell me his story. "It puts him in your power, Bunt, anybody who hears." But I must have had her in my power without knowing it. After she told me, she lay very still. Since we spent most of our time together in bed, I have few memories of her any other way. He has all those.

"Yes, yes—try." He held my grandmother offside like a vet holding a hurt animal. "Isn't it marvelous, there's nothing like it in the world." He breathed deep. "She is hunting necessity." He bent his head to hers.

"Go on, go,"he said. He was weeping joy, or sweating bright balm. It's *his* necessity, flashed over me. He wants her to do it for him. To show him the lengths to which people can go.

Nobody in the room could crack the text she'd quoted, though the donkey far down the table quoted a few wavering lines of what he said was the Twenty-fourth Psalm.

"Get a Bible." Leskel glanced at his watch.

Eagle Eye

All down the room, the guests murmured like people leaving a theatre. They were leaving us with our troubles. It was only polite.

I understand Buddy did go for a Bible . . . You can't do that, Batface, great as you are. Unless somebody in the office has already fed you all of it—which I doubt. Hear then, Corinthians, chapter ten, verse twenty-one: "You cannot drink the cup of the Lord and the cup of devils; you cannot partake of the Lord's table and the table of devils."

Meant for us human binaries, Batface. Not for you, who can partake of anything.

I hadn't stayed to hear. I had come to my senses at last and run after Maeve. Why wasn't she keeping us on anymore? Buddy? Me? The answer came to me in great spills of magnetic tape spiraling up through the house as I ran between its curling fountains, sidling at me anaconda from every corner. The machine of the past had vomited it.

I found her where I knew I would—at the terrarium door. She was standing with her back to me, pressed forward, her spread arms cradling the curved wall on either side, like a tiny Atlas holding the bubble of the world. Or an experimenter, about to step into space holding onto a glass-and-wrought-iron balloon.

The sneakers I'd changed to made their sneaker sound. A tremor in her shoulders told me she heard it. But in whatever yoga-plan she was breathing by, I had no place. I must have lost my place there long ago. For months on end, I had forgotten her myself. To me this was natural. Was it to her?

As I came nearer, she let go of the globe and wheeled to face me, arms at her side. Just before I got to her, moving slower because I was scared—she had her feet on solid floor, but I felt her teetering, as if she were going to jump somewhere—she reached behind her, slid open the terrarium door to an arc just wide enough to backstep into it, still facing me. Smiling humbly, deferent, she barred my way.

I let out my breath. In relief. I think the flesh of apartment dwellers never really forgets at what height it lives. Or not the child who is bred to it, warned when near windows, or grabbed away from them before language, his sight grilled with curlicued iron, or soft stone balustrade or glass, or nothing but nothing—between him and the people moving urgently down below. Down there is the empire. The eye is always making the magic, forbidden leap. In old dreams, I floated down plumb, my descent safe in the marble column of itself, to a slow melody. Heard at windowsills, when leaning awake. A tension, like silent decibels. One grew accustomed to it. A slight fear of heights. Like a slight fear of death.

I had never had it for her or Buddy, of course. They had had it for me. Now the balance had changed.

But she was in the safest place here. Heavy glass, aluminum banded at good close intervals. No access to the parapets—the only outside room that hadn't it. A small core of safety. Aluminum is such a joyously weightless metal, a cheap sunbeam in rain. I fell in love with modernity all over again, just looking at it.

"What a great idea, Maeve." And she is safe. No way to go except back to me where I am, feet planted on the same parquet pattern that has followed us through all the apartment houses.

She's standing just back of the glass wall that curves toward her from either side. The floor inside there must be some three inches higher, bringing her that much nearer my eye-level; when I first passed her height, years ago, I used to waggle a forefinger at her, senior to child.

Above her head, a dark fester of vines and leaf-faces pressed toward me through the glass.

"Even the door's curved, isn't it? That Claes is clever. Boy, what it must have cost." Brushing against her wrist as I put my palm against the doorframe, I find her arm rigid. She really means to keep me out. Of her lair? I can understand that.

"Oh, it cost."

No grin. In department-store days, there would have been.

"Maeve. What's between you and Buddy? . . . That I don't know, I mean."

"Nothing new."

"Something I should have known? And don't?" I

try to grin at her. "Or shouldn't have. The bathroom wall. Remember?"

She does look up, then. "Remember? The end of an era."

"The day I—" What had I done, really.

"You scared us. Me."

"How?"

"After that, I really did things Buddy's way. Before that, it was sometimes for myself."

"Your parties, you mean. Changing apartments. Your not going downtown."

"That the way you saw us? Only those three things?"

I shook my head like a swimmer. Second string. "Maybe it was me. The way I saw me. Between the two of you."

She shrugged. "People act on one another. A family. One day or another doesn't make the difference. Don't you mind."

"What am I minding? . . . You haven't yet said."

When she doesn't answer, I say "Maeve. Let me in, huh." I try to laugh it off. "Let me see your lair."

She looks up quick. Says nothing.

"After all, I am going to be an architect."

She put a palm up to my cheek. "Build well . . . No, stay where you are. I'll talk."

"Aw, come on." I become her child again. "We could sit on that bench in there."

On the far side of the terrarium, one of those iron cemetery benches had been poised, near what must be the new plants. Thin airy ones, spreading their lace; they couldn't weigh that much. At each point in the wall where there was a metal stave, Claes had bracketed it with a speared oval teardrop frame in filigree, in the center of each of which there was a piece of milky glass —amber or lavender or green, and in one or two, an old streaked mirror; he had copied what the eighteenth century called a repose. It did make me feel a child again. In front of a secret garden. Out of those fairybooks I'd hated, but wanted to believe in.

"No. No."

She's not lucid here. At this point, it stops. Here at this door. And here is where I'm no longer a child.

"Okay. Give."

"You make me feel so good. So normal. Just to hear your slang."

"A convenience. That's what I am. You're brown-nosing me." But I couldn't make her smile. I touched her hair. "Since when Kwan Yin."

"Since."

Depression became her; she looked younger for it. But it sat on her cheeks like rouge on a corpse's. On the one corpse I'd seen.

"You look like him. Like Granpa MacNeil. I never saw it before."

"You only saw him dead." She reached up to touch the spot between my eyebrows, where the Hindus put a red dot. Or the ash goes, on Ash Wednesday.

"I used to be afraid your chin would turn out like hers. Like a cat's."

"Maybe it will yet. My mother'll never make a Park Avenue wheelchair lady, though, no matter what Buddy does. People should lead their lives to their natural outcome. She's doing it. I don't mind her anymore. Not like Buddy hoped."

"But you left, just now, when she—"

"No, I did it for myself. I'm doing that now. Learning it."

"For yourself, Maeve?"

"I can only do it here."

The globe was like a rival. Into which she would recede.

"You're a quick learner."

Joke. But she shrank. I don't have to imitate Buddy. I already sound like him. She made a movement. I saw she wanted in. I needed to delay her. That's all the vibes said.

"How'd you come to build this thing?"

"I came here for the city, you know. When I was young."

"Well?"

"I wanted to look at the city again."

"Again?"

"Like from the Amenia porch."

She had never said anything like that to me. In my whole life. Like that sounded. "And can you?" I wanted to know too. It would be something I could hold onto.

She looked down, hunted. It was the simplicity that scared me. "Oh, Bunt. I see so much."

Husky-voiced. A woman I'd never seen before. A woman. Making me see how in all the girl-wrestling I'd maybe never seen any of them—right. How they chain themselves to each other—after we chain them. Be careful, Jasmin was saying to me. Your mother's voice has death in it. But it's not too late.

"Strange, how I can *talk* to you," Maeve said. "Why is that?"

I couldn't tell her yet; it would choke me. Kangaroo.

"You shouldn't have come back," my mother said.

"Why not?"

"I don't want to talk."

"Maybe I do." I took her by the wrists. Doing any of this wasn't going to make me feel any bigger. But this was the audience I had. "Tell me, Maeve—has Buddy always given the parties around here?"

She went limp. Only a little. I'd only slapped her gently, with her life. I let her go.

"You shouldn't have come back."

"You're telling me I'm not worth anything. That's not nice." I could smile at that whimsy from a world where the rainbows weren't barbed wire yet. She looked ravaged enough to be my mother. I was old enough. "I'm away from you, from you both. Without having to be away."

"How do you mean, Bunty?"

"I learned a lot over there, sure. But not what Buddy thought. Not in the galleries only. Walking the streets, watching Europe. And in the bars, with my friends."

When we talked, no matter about millions of things,

no matter what, underneath it was always about them back here—and us. Versus us. They were in possession of our childhoods. From a hundred thousand miles away—three times round the globe and over, they held us fast.

"It was in Paris I learned it most. In the restaurants. Watching the kids and the parents—once I ate a whole dinner watching a couple with a two-year-old. Her grandparents owned the place, but she sat up and ate like a little granny anyway—she knew she was watched. Oh there was love going around; when the grandpa served me the melted butter I thought he'd drown me in it, looking at her sideways. And the grandma came out of the kitchen like under a spell. But they were all so cool about it, the baby most of all." I couldn't believe it, whatever it was. "And when dinner was over, a little white dog jumped out from beneath the cloth. From the baby's lap. And in their own family restaurant." It knew, too, whatever was being taught there in front of my eyes. It was the coolest of all.

"In Asia, too," I said. "Though there it was too much. When they were poor. The parents were teaching them how to be. How to *be* the underdog. I won't buy that."

I'd interested her. Fishing for her, skeining. Somebody had to. And could do it only with the truth. She'd spread her arms against the curve of her lair—but she was listening. "What do you mean—I was telling you you're not worth anything?"

"They've got other things wrong over there. But

149

I could feel it in the streets. In the parks especially.
Maybe it's wrong. Maybe it only leads to armies in
another way. But I wanted it."

"What?" Maeve said. "What *did* you want?"

They'd never really asked that, she and Buddy. Only
thought they had.

"A girl said it to me. She was going back to Boston
to teach in a nursery, because of it, she said. She was
going to try to teach them it. Monica, her name was."
She was still coming down, when she said it to me. I'd
held onto her while she screamed and huddled. Sex
helped. I was sick on my own, though I hadn't had
a thing. Tired of my world-dwarfing, I huddled too.

"She said it was too late for you to teach us
obligation," I said. "She said you only taught us love."

"Smart," my mother said. "You're smart."

"Let's make it a rule," I said. "Not to say that to
each other. Ever again. A family rule."

Maeve looked up at me. "Too late for that. Your
girl was right . . . Bunty dear. Go away and leave me
for a bit, then."

"Leave you?"

She stretched out her hands. "Be."

How seductive her voice was—and not for me. I
knew how hard I had to fish for her. What I couldn't
figure was how. There was some secret to the terrarium.
A bloody secret garden—somewhere.

Holding onto her hands, not wanting to let them
go—or was she holding me?—treading water for a time,

150

I cast my eyes here, there. "School starts you becoming a person, Maeve, that's all." Her apologetic, blue-eyed boy, swinging arms with her. "I became one to myself. You two didn't, to me. You stayed where you were. In my mind." I leaned closer, close. "Tell me, then. About Buddy. It can't be so terrible."

"Only to me. And it's no secret."

"Only to me, Maeve."

"What good is it, if I tell you how Buddy lies to himself? I can't tell you mine." She gave me her strange, transparent smile, as if I must be seeing through her lips to them.

"He digs being rich, you mean."

"For me," she said, with the smile. "Only for me." And she looked away from me, at the terrarium.

What's there, what's there? The jewels had been. That she doesn't wear. The Kwan Yin that he began looking at art with. And when he knew better, discarded, leaving it with Maeve. The suit of armor, if we still had it. Disposed of after some jokey guest stuck a pair of sunglasses on it. It's all here, what she came to the city for. Why weigh it on him?

"Generosity can be a disease." Maeve turned up my palms, staring at them. "That doctor tells Buddy it's a way of possessing people. Buddy told me."

Jannie should know. I saw him in the launderette. With Jasmin's check in hand. Holding his face out to her, like a check.

"And what did Buddy say?"

"He laughed, and said 'Jannie's not a Jew.' Your father's just as sick as they say I am. Only he's a success at it."

She raised her chin high. I saw her mother in it. I saw her natural outcome. Or thought I did. And could love her for it. In a way she never taught me to. "Oh, Maeve." I held my arms out, to her shabbiness. I hugged her to me, a bag of bones that had no more demands in them. What did it matter whether those demands were hers or Buddy's—she had no more of them. I felt it in her—the emptiness of those who demand nothing from others anymore. Or not from themselves.

Or who tell you the stories that help them dwarf the world.

I let her go. Watching carefully. Standing near. Somewhere—there was a brink.

"I've a confession to make. I gave one of your coats to a girl."

If she asked which coat, it meant that she could still be dragged back.

"Did you. I hope she needed it."

"She reminded me of you a little." I suppose Jannie would say that's why I get the girls I get.

But it wasn't merely the way the two of them felt to my arms—smallboned, downbeat. It was when Dina spoke of Felipe. Oh, I believed in her tale of the sphincter muscle. But I could tell the reason she and he hung together must be different. Why wouldn't he come here? What if she ripped off houses like this because she

152

wanted to? Why would he rather mug? What did they hang onto each other for? What was their joint sadness?

"Did she. She live near?"

She said it absently, the way she had asked about schoolmates when I interrupted her, peering down meanwhile at a task. A glass globe, decorated and almost finished now? Why did I think that? What did it lack?

"In the park." I said. Absently.

"The park." Maeve stared through her glass lair and out the other side. "I'd like to live there."

"Maeve. Maeve." I'd been with as many way-out people as anybody. I couldn't take it in her. "Maeve—let's go get some gormay."

"*Gour*-may, it is," my mother said. Half-laugh, half-sob. "I found out." And all her charm came back to me. Her wild, whirl-on-a-heel intentness when she wanted something. She would get it too, like always. Unless I got there ahead of her.

I followed her stare. "Your plants—your new plants. They don't seem to be doing very well. Even though Claes watered them."

"Oh, they'll do," she said. Staring at them as if they were shelves. With her death on them.

They'll say now that she was telling me. Asking me for help. Directing me toward it. But I don't believe it. She had it all worked out. She hadn't asked me to come back. And had taken all precautions. The key was at her waist.

She was only gambling on when.

Eagle Eye

You guess things because of what you are. In Maine once, I knew a local boy who couldn't tell his left from his right—and walked more unerring in the woods because of it. My habit is maybe a city one. I'm always miming space with my elbows—or a cock of the head, a stretching of ears—anything handy. I follow architecture with my body. Skyscrapers don't do anything for me; I just stand tall. The Taj Mahal made me spread my fingers—Siva Siva. And certain parts of Italy put me in knots. Or tempted me to fly. Jasmin was onto it. "Think of me as Borromini Tower," she said once. And leaned back.

"Buddy bought the farm," my mother said. "Our farm. Watch out. He thinks he did it for you."

Funny how just as I began to catch onto what the lair was—to mime its space to myself, plotting it mentally with my feet, getting the feel of it in my arms, receiving its message like a cable I couldn't read yet—my mother began to tell me what she thought was the story of her life. Just as I was only half-listening; maybe she felt that. We talk best, Bats, to those who're no longer listening.

I was observing the plants. Dark-snouted, the nearer ones, healthy velvet, clambering toward us, opening their broad throats. Screaming. If I could only tune in.

"Don't take a house from him," Maeve said. "You'll never get it right for him. Or if you do, you'll only be its secretary: Secretary to the house. And he'll move on. *He'll* be doing it down at the office. While everybody's watching the house. He's too smart for us. That's one time he tells the truth.

The plants in the rear—high, graceful aureoles new from the greenhouse—were already only a faded lace, scarcely breathing, their broad skirts drooping, as if a squeezing hand was at their roots. At the Folies Bergère, I'd seen a mock ballet of Circe—twining green sirens, oldish women most of them, kicking and cavorting in and out of painted cloth waves, from behind each of which an iridescent serpent-arm rose and pulled them down. All done in black light. The plants back there looked as if they too were in stage-light, on another plane. The cemetery bench was pushed near them. And close to it—the Kwan Yin was back. Inside.

"Buddy's afraid to be rich. He has to have somebody to lay it on. But the peacock has to stand very still. Take his money, if you have to. I earned it. But get away somewhere. To that Paris, if it pleases you."

"You can't earn it for me," I said. "Not going to war taught us that."

I tucked my elbows tight against my ribs. Architecturally, the terrarium was speaking to me. But a real terrarium is for plants, I thought. All moisture, no air. Or not much. It's not for the animal kingdom. Even a peacock wouldn't want in. Not for long.

"He wanted to give me the farm. He planned on it. I thought, yes, maybe I could stand on the porch there. And look at my life. But he wouldn't be there standing with me. Equal. He won't do it with you either. Even poor old Blum agrees with that."

. . . But I'm young. And I'm the son . . . True, Bud hadn't mentioned taking her up there. When he talks of her, he never gets her quite right—I saw that. But he couldn't be the ogre she made of him either—I knew that. "What's Blum got to do with it?"

"When I went down there, that once, to the opening, I made friends with her again. She was his girl for a long time once; did you know?"

"Now that I think of it." I hadn't, much.

The Kwan Yin I'd mistaken for Maeve was in position again; I could see its coif, bent. Anyone who sat on the bench would be looking at its face. On the other side of the bench—another head, too high for an occupant of the bench to pat easily. The Chinese lion glared at me resignedly; porcelain never believes its own expression. But always knows its value. This one was a beauty. Like mismated companions, those two. She must have dragged them both back.

"She still is," Maeve said. "Now and then. Buddy's a generous man. He doesn't like to see the money go out of the family, but he's generous. Every one of the girls he's had since, has had a house built for her. When he moved on."

"Maeve." It stood to reason. That a man wouldn't have just one. But within a family, it's always a revelation. "Did you always know?"

"No, but should I mind, really? I'm the one he never left. Blum says he hasn't anybody now. And my house, he's grown to love it. Look at it."

156

Did she like it, didn't she. From her expression I couldn't tell.

"What about you?—did you ever?"

"Once. But he lived in the suburbs. We couldn't keep it up."

It was chilling, of course. To find out they hadn't lived their lives for me. Still, I had been kept. For tonight.

"Can I stand like you? Like this?" I sidled—and suddenly I was backed up against the globe, spread-eagled against it with my hand halfway from my sides, like hers. I made myself laugh at her. "Gives you a feeling you're off the floor." The sliding door was between us now. With a chink of light on the open side. My side.

"If we'd moved to the suburbs, it might have worked out. I might have got out. But he wasn't a city man. Living in a Bronxville hotel. Temporarily. The Gramatan, the one that closed a while back. When I saw the notice of that, I—but of course we *didn't* move."

. . . In the bathroom, way back. Could I have sensed it, somewhere between the elbows? . . .

"You were going to leave Buddy?"

"I needed time to. He was negotiating for a seed farm; he wanted us to live on it. You see its name now in all the garden stores." She said it dreamily. "Maybe I would have. But this way—we broke up. I felt guilty for a long time."

I didn't ask her which way. Maybe she saw my face. I wouldn't bank on it.

"He wasn't a city man, that was only why. You

mustn't think that Buddy and I haven't anything in com . . . —that we haven't had—it may be hard to see now . . . but once."

I knew what they had. You see it any age, anywhere; none of us our age knows how to get out of it. In all actuarial probability I'll inherit the tendency; the margin of error otherwise is very small. She and Buddy have a hell of a lot in common, even without our long line of houses, the pile of stocks and bonds that must go with it, and me like a sick-and-sorry Cupid on top. Or the farm, that will go blindly, serenely from one owner to the next, with all its brambles and cows. She and Buddy—my parents the Bronsteins—they dug each other's lies. They tell each other the same world-dwarfing stories. Call it love; people do.

"Buddy show you those peepholes?" Maeve said. "When we came here, he showed me the one in the hall. 'Peek.' he said. I did, and what-do-you-know, I saw my life. And the house I should build for it."

She bites her lip just like Buddy does. "You think badly of us?"

"I don't, Ma." I'd dropped that, at their suggestion when I was six.

She looked me full in the face. Put her hands out to me, forsaking her wall. "What we gave you, I'm sorry it was only love."

It was then I jumped. Into the terrarium. Lightly, as I knew I must. Dropping on all fours. That way I figured to equalize any shock. Of my weight. The step

up had been about three inches. I had cleared it. My
weight after a summer of no swimming is one-seventy.
Nothing trembled in this floating filigree in which I
had landed. What had I expected? Floor was floor under
my knees and palms. Balsa. Good show, Claes. Yet my
elbows hugged my sides, dreaming their stresses and
strains.

A border of earth, flower-box wide, circled the wall.
No plants showed, but it had been heavily watered.
There must be a run-off for seepage below. Where had
the drains been in the hanging gardens of
Babylon?—holes in the stone itself maybe, savoring the
precious stuff like a camel's gut. There was provision
for violet light here, and up from the floor near the
door a separate switch box which I opened. A Murray
Load Center, all trim and well-housed. That was wise.
I closed it.

Clinging to the doorframe, my mother leaned in
at me, whispering like a gargoyle that dared not scream.
As if even air counted here.

When I moved, she moaned.

I stood up slowly from the ankles, to a kneebend,
keeping my center of gravity holy, like an acrobat. Only
my body was smart. I still hadn't guessed.

Slowly I inched toward the grouping at the bench.

"Don't. Not any nearer. *Bunt.*"

"Where is it, then." I turned, slow-motion. A gas-
cock, my stupid head was looking for. Or a small egg
of metal, set to ignite. After all I'd been brought up

on explosions, rocket-flares, house timbers rising like feathers and settling again in the television air. With the people running ahead, clouds behind them, their faces stretched like hers.

"Everywhere." A puzzled whisper, more lucid than mine.

"Is it in the plants?"

A nod. Hands wrung white. When I moved again, one covered her mouth. "Hold still. *Wait.* Please wait." She covered her eyes.

I felt behind me, in one of the pots. The plant, set in spongy florist's stuff, had almost no roots. The rest of the pot, iron and about eighteen inches in diameter, was filled with stones, mixed with disks, machined, and regular. I palmed one, inching it out. An ordinary old-fashioned kitchen-scale iron weight, marked with a "5." I didn't need to examine the other pots. All close in a ring, and all as large. My hand had spoken to my head. Finally.

As a child, after all, it was only *falling* from windows that I'd been warned of. But in the apartment-house dream, sometimes, slow as blood-hum, the wall sinks away, and down.

I turned my head. An oddly intimate grouping—a bench, a lion, and a statue. All with one thing in common. And now me. And I had it too.

No odder than any fire-escape family. On a hot night. A short, intent man, say, and a thin, cool woman. The wicker stool the son always sat on. And the son,

of course, the last to be added. They always settled themselves before he was allowed there. To be alone there
was forbidden, though he had done it. Mornings, when
only the maid. Now it was night. And we three are gazing
out, into the central park of our longings, that ends
for some on Fifth Avenue, on the far side. But we are
together still. We are each of us pulling our weight.

Like now.

"Maeve . . . look at me."

She'd never stopped. She shook recognition into
her eyes. We were maybe four yards apart. Less. I held
out my arms . . . I had a right to know, I thought. But
did I? In the years to come, I'll fathom it . . .

"Come, Maeve. Join me? Us."

She scraped her thighs with her nails. Agony is
simple. A skull trampled into pavement. A woman lug-
ging weights into her house. A man watching them.

. . . You've guessed it, haven't you Batface . . .

She stretched her arms toward mine. Keening is
a throw-back sound. "I daren't. Add my weight."

So we had trapped each other, she and I.

"It was only for me," she said. "Only for me."

"Is it to maximum?"

"Past. It must be. Days ago. Those plants. . . . Bunt?
How did you know to come?"

How had I?

"I had a loss."

I started to walk back.

"No! Don't move suddenly. Hold still."

If I did, what would I hear?

"Let me call the fire department maybe. Or get a rope."

"No sweat. I'll bet it's okay." How violent her images were, of how to get through normal life. Machinery instead of muscle, that's the real violence; sanity is not involved. "You added the weight day by day, is that it?" Hour by hour?

"Whenever I could. I look through the peephole. And then."

Her voice was so dry. It drew my respect.

"Right. I'd watch that earth-border after this, though. Against too much watering." And seepage from rain.

"Just get over here. Please."

But when I lifted a toe, she went white. "Can you jump?"

I thought of all the old architecture I knew. But I was adrift in their world now. Of reinforced concrete.

"No sweat." I smiled at her, humoring. "Not for a swimmer." A sprint, and a little flying jump up and over onto the other floor-level, nothing for my long legs.

And all the time, I was sure that the world would hold. "Okay, hon. Stand back from the door."

I took a look at the apartment from there. The huge Rothko glowed red, descending into orange, then to a nude band I couldn't entirely see. I raised myself on toe, leaned forward.

And Doughty shot past her through the door. Slid
to a braking stop on the glossy floor. Snapped at Lion,
dismissed him with a sniff of recognition, and sauntered
to earth. Nosed it, trotting this new globe full circle.
On the far side, he stopped, looking at us. Dogs relate
to posture. In us. Suddenly he sprang in the air, yipping
at his own behind, galumphing round and round, up
and down, with mock-snaps over his shoulder at us,
fawning for the ball I must have somewhere, prancing
high again, in the antic glee of the good animal who
knows the difference between real wrong and the mis-
chief we will love him for. At the far end he stopped
short, growling. Faced us over his shoulder. Not a growl
—I'd never heard a dog make that sound. A cajoling
whine. A cringing whimper. At the enemy he can't see.

How much does a Great Dane weigh? His puzzled,
dowager face asked me it, while his back legs scrabbled
a little, sensitive one second before I was, to the canting
of the floor.

Maybe earthquakes begin like that. Nothing savage
at first, or open. No cracks you can see. An undertow.
Your sense of perpendicular is even tickled. Like anything important that happens, the feel is partly sexual.
Like fear.

Maeve screamed. My name. Or I'd have stood there.
Back of me, under, I felt the floor yawning away from
my heel. I dug in the toes of my sneakers, sprinted
up the incline that tilted in front of me—in real falling,
the dream isn't of *down,* but of *up*—grabbed for one

of the aluminum struts that had buckled forward, swung there while the strut slowly bent—from the Mark of Zorro, Douglas Fairbanks flashed me, I swear it—and kneeing inward with all my strength I landed, sprawled. Maeve helped me up. I held her, slumped in my arms. Behind us we heard the crack.

When Jannie and my father came up, the first to come running, I still held her, they say, lifted, her head and feet dangling, like some girl I had dragged in from the sea.

I remember Jannie. He was ahead of Buddy, and his need shines always in his face. I approve of that. He'd already run such a distance with that life-story of his behind him, a bundle that whether he walks or runs hits him regularly in the back.

Anyway, I handed her to him. Right in his arms. While Buddy stood by. Buddy's newsboy face would haunt me, but I couldn't help that.

"People get lost," I said.

I hear Buddy wanted to go in after Doughty but was restrained. Poor Doughty's nails didn't have much purchase on the balsa; maybe that frightened him. He could have made it; the terrarium had sagged to a point and then stopped. But he cowered at the border, his

164

four feet clamped in earth. A bright fireman got him,
though not until the police were called too. After they'd
sent in the tear gas, the ladderman got Doughty—with
a grappling hook, it looked like. Whatever they use on
us. I saw the dog's arched neck rear above the battle-
smoke like a Delacroix horse; two of the buckling metal
staves crossed under it like bayonets. Gravel he was kicking up soared in high arcs and fell, slow as tracer bullets
—from old movies. I could hear the dum-dum bullets,
softnosed, exploding on impact—that people thought
we had outlawed. And this was only one house.

When I slouched off, the police were already calling
the demolition experts. I could have told them the terrarium wasn't going to fall any further, of itself. As
proved the case. It was to hang there for two months
while a wreckage crew with the will and means was
sought for—the area-way wasn't very large. And while
the Fifth Avenue Association protested the crowds that
came to view. They came like they still did, I heard,
for that house the Weathermen blew up on West
Eleventh Street. Maybe they took the day off and visited
both. Our globe could have hung there like at Pisa, or
at Venice, or Agra, where the ruined angles still hold
for a long, long time. They could have let it hang there
in its milky colors, like a warning from Fifth Avenue,
to those fancy highrisers that watch us from the
Palisades. We could have propped it up, and it could

165

have stayed there for people to brood on. In the mornin'
an' the evenin', as the song says. A warning and a miracle.
An opal bad-luck piece.

But I saw how the clear and present danger en-
nobled every official face. We build for ruin here, we
don't save for it. And the flat would be sold. And I
knew I didn't want to be an architect.

When we begin to slouch off—my crowd, our age,
call us what you want—it starts a long way back, in the
way the bones handle, the clothes and the gait, the voice.
A kind of pussy-footing, with insolence. For all our torn
fates. Throwing it away, onka-bonka. Throwing it all
away. Yet khaki is still so boss for us. Such a camouflage.
I was wearing army surplus myself. When I left the
wall I was leaning on, they never saw me go.

I went into the armory-room, to get my head clear.
Quiet place, leather-padded for history to be comfortable here, old-blotter walls, air dim as a museum afternoon, in the wrong wing. The collection was a laugh,
but I liked it. Halberds and vizors, musketry on a wall.

I never wanted to be a summer soldier. Or a winter
one. Above Seventy-sixth Street, I heard a passenger
plane whining toward nirvana. People are the bombs
now. Hold your breath, the air's bleeding as they pass
through. All soldiers are the same now, in their sphinc-
ters and in their khaki brains. And all lonely slouchers,
walking sentry for the world. There's no leaving it.

I went to the nearest bathroom and vomited up
the war.

166

◧

The gourmet you can get at night in the downtown financial district is extraordinary. You can sit in the one glow-worm hash-house that keeps open for policemen and other derelicts, have a western omelet, and watch dawn creep up the spine and structure of the world. The financial one. And the moral one. At four AM, their minarets tend to combine at the top. Buddy wanted to sit at a table, but the guy at the grill said, "Counter service only, buddy."

"Come here often?" Bunty said. "Seems to know you." He glommed in the mirror at his own cruel face, on which the red beard was beginning to blush.

"We have our own commissary."

"I'll serve us," Bunty said. "My pal's beat." He settled his father at a table, and brought back the food. Buddy had his head in his hands. That was normal here. They sat for a while, until Buddy could take a sip of coffee. When he had downed half a cup, his head came up.

"Westerns are the best in these joints." This reversal of roles gave Bunt no surface joy. But at the bottom of himself, an imp of Kilkenny screwed out a smile. "Come on, eat something."

His father ate. In the window, the view bloomed like a series of cathedrals walking toward them along the river's edge. They were on a stretch of sludge looking northeast up the harbor, at the outcroppings which hid the inland city. Two of the nearest towers were like marlinspikes, half-hitched to the sky.

"Very good." Buddy made no move to go.

"Funny, how no matter what they build down here, it ends up looking maritime."

"All made-land, this part." His father pushed at a crust on his plate.

Two workmen rolled in, fresh-faced and far-eyed, as if they had come up out of the water itself.

"Place must serve the crews on the Trade Center. They work early, sometimes all night. Port Authority dispensation. Or the Mayor."

This was the most his father had said since the police had made them leave the apartment. Gas seepage, they said, and maybe watersoaked cables. You folks better go to a hotel for the night, hah? Money's no problem here, the lieutenant's left eye said to the patrolman he was leaving on guard. As he took Buddy's donation. All smooth. Except that Buddy wouldn't go to a hotel.

"Mayor's a pal of yours, huh?"

"We can see this area. From my secretary's office."

"Blum?"

Buddy nodded. The food had given him color.

"She has a good view, huh. The best."

For a liar, his father had steady eyes. "The whole office has a good view, Bunty."

"Which way do *you* face?" He couldn't help it if he sounded like that actor talking to old Von Stroheim from the opposing battlement.

Buddy had his elbows on the table. "Everywhere." He spoke from behind his fists. "We have the whole floor." He shrugged. He took no joy in that now, the shrug said. But a newsboy from Brooklyn twitched one corner of his mouth.

"One whole floor up there?" Through the cafe's other window they could see the building complex he recognized from slides, a dull safe-deposit gray, up against the Strozzi Palace of the Federal Reserve. "You must own a bank."

The sky outside was scudding to a wind. Going to be one of those rough equinoctial days.

"Maybe we do. You never came downtown to see."

One of these days that came anytime of the year, any country. The waves were whipping a little, past these buildings that were all of silver, no matter what the dawn was saying.

"Maybe we should all go to live down there. Maybe we should of, long time back." He felt sick. Glad.

"You might get lost down there, friend. Your last letter was sent to two offices back." Buddy put his palms on the table, to stop their tremor.

He means what kind of a son am I, can't remember his father has an office at One Chase.

Listen Buddy. What's this all of a sudden you been holding the fort and I'm the shirk? You approved of me not going, all along the line. You all but connived. Or would have, if my number had come up. Pulling strings, like Gramps did for Uncle Charlie in the last one—oh yeah, I heard.

Eagle Eye

The greaser was looking at them; the place was filling up.

"I go round the world, Buddy, the whole world," he said. "And I don't get lost. Only here." He got up and went to the counter to pay. One of the two workmen who had come in first was joshing the other. "Pay for your coffee just because you're my boss, ah c'mon." He winked at the counterman. "Section boss he is, since yesterday. Nah c'mon, bigtime." He paid.

The money in his pocket sluiced through his fingers. He paid.

Buddy was already at the door. Below his own eye level, his father's shoulder was the same substantial bulwark it had always been. He pressed a hand on it and opened the door.

Going up the hill to the Chase, Buddy took his arm. He seemed to need it. A strange sensation. He held his own arm stiff. Available without seeming to be. "Sure you don't want to go to a hotel?"

No answer. *Why are we going to the office?*—his father had said, still white about the gills, as they left the apartment, handing the keys to the guard—*We are going to the office because that is where I feel safe.*

When they reached the Plaza, Buddy disengaged his arm. To one side of the patterned stone well in the center, a huge white plaster thingum, gaily striped in black, froggied its open spaces at them, galumphing on the gray air. "The new Dubuffet. Like it?"

Public games. Two of the early morning populace passed under it, mute and dogfaced.

"Looks as if it's kidding the place." The town had opened its streets to these outcroppings, and closed its eyes. "Thingum-*lingam*," that card Jasmin had said, passing one.

"Rockefeller took a lot of flak for it."

Flak. On a civvy tongue. It scraped him. It violated old movies. He had no other right.

Going up in the elevator, his ears clicked. The elevator brinked. After Europe's, it had the self-assurance of a plane. He stepped from it, eyes wide as a blind man's. Buddy led him to a gilt-marked door.

"Q. Bronstein," Bunty said. On his own passport it was spelled out. "I like that."

"Get a lot of mileage out of that Q."

A lot, a lot. A little, a lot. A son, a son. His father's linear reality walked before them, like a duck.

"You didn't eat, did you. You can eat here." Buddy held out a small key. "Blum had it made for me at Tiffany."

Gold. He had no interest in the inscription. "What do I do with it?"

"Open up." Buddy was panting.

The door gave without fuss. No alarms here. His father passed under his arm, stumbling like a man coming up out of a submarine. Murmuring "Show you later," he shucked coat and hat on a desk, went in the door marked Q.B., and came out with a couple of pills in his palm, and a glass. "Seconal. Want one?"

"No thanks."

"C'mon then." He downed a pill. "This stuff won't

take for a quarter-hour yet. I'll hold off on the other one. Give you the short tour."

"Okay." He saw Buddy was still trembling.

The place was quiet as a dead beehive. All shades were at weekend half-mast. He had walked into a part of his childhood which he had forgotten—the Saturday half-day office—and knew at once he would miss forever, if he took no care. Limegreen quiet. Clerks here or not here, but all with lives folded like locust-wings behind them. Kept well back of what was needed here. Cherry voices, thick with orderliness. All tame ghosts, ready for Monday. The telephones sentient; no real death here. Night coming on, with its uptown complications, but there's a chance you could stay; there's a cot in the washroom. And a couch. He and his father had done it once; he must have been about five. Brooklyn, and a death. They had come here to escape the hysterical drawstrings of the house. And to be where Buddy had to be in the morning. Even with his grandmother dead, he could feel his father lapped in that earthly satisfaction. The letters on the door then were his grandfather's: A.B. "In Abraham's bosom," his father said, bringing him a play pad and pencils. "Yes, it's good here." He had already half-learned to read from the lettering on such pads, and ledgers and bill-forms. The office lingo exchanged above his head stuck there like the "hundreds and thousands" candies he always got here, which congregated in his palm, mixing their tiny colors with his dirt, before he got them down. There was a word in the washroom, not quite rubbed out, what was it? "Give

172

that Caliban of a cleaner his time and goodbye," Abe
had said. On the moved-out cot, waves of selling and
buying rocked him to sleep as neatly as the painted cross-
stitching on his home nursery towel. Above his head,
on the darkish, diplomaed wall, the word, "Actuary"
glimmered like a furl from Abe's feather-pen, which
stood on the desk in a bell of shot, and had come from
a time called the sesquicentennial.

And all night long, he woke to watch the desk, hoping that the beautiful birds of chance might fly out of
their pigeonholes.

You never liked offices, Betts. You drank to
get out of them and "into" life, as you said—and
got jammed halfway. I think you never tasted an
office young enough. To feel the blood-urge when
the beehive is humming, and people are going hap-
pily out of their minds with the business that keeps
them sane. And porky with eating that's paid for.
And sexed, with the sweet pinch of ass and swell
of cockfight that underwrites all deals.

You never felt the mysticism of those after-
hours down here or the Sunday ones, which comes
of having the power to support a church without
ever entering it, because rich men pass through the
eye of the needle every time the telephone rings,
and afterwards there is always a little typist-perfume
lingering in the world of big ideas. But you'll have
to plug it in. Give old Batface its bit of barmecide.

Funny, that until I pushed in that office door

173

after so long, I never thought of the place. Though it's no secret to us that the man must confront the childhood. For the words in the washroom to burn up again in all their flaming colors, and the Calibans to crowd around us with their steamy brushes. And for the hundredfold innocences to roll again in the grundgey palm.

I pushed in that door—and out flew all the beautiful, sorry birds of chance.

When that happens, you can speak to a father in his lair.

We'd made the tour I could see he thought was such a big one. If you could walk with me now on the periphery of this so-called office, you would be tracing a high, miniature counterpart of this island, and its escarpments, the size of watch parts from up here, connecting on and on.

"Mainland can't be told from island any more, can it," I said. "You sure can see that from here."

He liked that. I could see the world-dwarfing glitter in his eyes, as if you could cap an eye with gold, the way you can a tooth.

People in the street know that mainland-island bit by now. I made my naked eye-lens zoom down there, so that in my mind I saw them as I wanted to—just as knowing in their shabbiness. He had his mainland, I mine.

Inside the place here, there's a real heartland of

rooms that provision for nearly everything; you can imagine them connecting with lives outside, on and on. I like best the kitchen commissary that supplies everybody, from the hall large enough to entertain a government, to the director's boardroom, to the coffee shop where the collars wilt from white to blue. I could tell from the cookery smells that there were Helgas here.

We peeped into the circular room that is a small stock exchange, where I could see how it would be on a business day—men crowded, beef-heads and lantern-jaws, curly and bald, diplomaed and rough diamond, hook-nose and North Shore pug, all at the round table-trough, while the lights jabbed on and off, on the big wall. It would be like a horse-auction I saw once in Brittany. You would never catch the flicker of the eye that says, "Buy!" Or the death-loll of the tongue that says sell.

Nearby, a door said Comparisons. Didn't ask what meant; didn't want to ask him anything more for a long while. Besides, I could figure it; the sellers and buyers both will want to know how well they've managed it. Money's not so different from other constructions. Elbow-space. The pigeonhole pockets opening and shutting, while the brick builds in the bank vaults. And when all the plumbing's in, government to government, state to state—and all the wires that you can teletype sugar and wheat and other futures on; when you've bonded people and their mutuals for the best tax shelters, how different is the lingo from Corinthians? You've got your cathedral. With a little bit of Borromini at the top if you want it, to make a girl lean back.

I'd tell him that later. Someday. In my own way.

You take much Seconal these days?—I was about to ask him, when he one-upped me. He opened the door on you. Batface.

I didn't know you at first. The thingum he calls "the Zebel thing" is in front.

"Like it?" he said. Computer banks are getting smaller all the time. For the same performance. Still, for our needs—size gives confidence. Never thought we'd get Zebel though. To dress it up. This is the front office, you know. You and I came in the back."

How you can have a front and back to a near-perfect circle, is Buddy's lookout. I walked over to the great screen and flattened my palm on it. Not aluminum. Steel. Trying to look like a cosmic spider web, but only fifteen-foot high and within the building code. Shining through the plate-glass entry, Zebel's metal mesh winked at the populace through dozens of light-slots, each one hooded in the very shape of the Rockefeller eye. Spiders of the world, unite!—I thought. You can do better; Art gets smaller all the time. But I liked Zebel; he was a man with a joke.

"Good as the Dubuffet anytime, Buddy," I said. "Both of them understand Americans." Zebel must've known my father wasn't ready yet. For any flak. No matter; he did the right thing. You can't hide a computer with art.

176

I stepped behind the Zebel to the good, clean space where the computer is. You are your own description, Batface, in magnetic light. And thoughts that get larger, all the time.

"Oh, God," I said. "Oh God, god." And a 7090. "The Lord is my shepherd." Here you are.

"Had a course in them once, didn't you." He was yearning with pleasure. I'd admired something he had.

He didn't even mind that I knelt.

I was at Betts' grave again. His silent, magnetic grave. Knowing better now why I'd chosen his to visit, out of all those I could have touristed to. Vietnam, if I'd wanted to. People could do that all through the war, like vivandières. But I could never see any percentage in visiting the dead. For either of us. Yet I'd taken a plane and a bus to get to it—and a ramshackle limousine that rattled like a paddy-wagon and then broke down, leaving me to walk two miles unhelmeted, as if this was the right way that transportation to a grave should end.

Back here where no beetles were honing, Batface told me why I had done it. My father's computer could tell me that without being asked. Betts taught me what Tufts had taught him. From bicycle to bicycle, I learned it, under the Babbidge-light the stars were sending us from the past, while we rode through people, machines and nature—all waiting to be hemmed in. In the lab, sweating next to me over the holy buttons, he taught me. The way Tufts taught him. With no words, and never an embrace. That's why I went to New Delhi.

To give him his percentage. He taught me obligation, Buddy. I thought it was love.

"Yeah, Buddy, I had a course. Like to find out someday, how this one ticks." I put my hand on a familiar part of it. New Batface, larger and meaner to feed, but still the same.

"You would, huh." Buddy put his glass of water down; he hadn't taken the second capsule yet. He was glowing with a look I knew of old, without recognizing until now where he got it from. Old Abe's—when a wayward boy was found to be still a possibility.

"Yeah. I thought I was over it. But I was lying to myself."

He stared absently at the capsule. When you've taken a hundred of those, they're like aspirin, like speed or anything. Or the wee, gummy pipe that Jasmin put me onto, once—a souvenir, brought to her with all the fixings, by a girl she'd nursed with in Hongkong. I suppose that not getting as gone as she did for those four hours, put me into the terror I have of it. I can't stand to see anybody I like put themselves out. While I sit there alive-oh, and the double-bloody minutes, theirs and yours, go nihil-nihil down the windowpane.

"Got something else to show you, Bunty, something else. You don't mind?"

"Mind? No, I don't mind." I minded his humbleness, though. Like his letter, theirs, it wasn't to me, but to my youth—which made a nothing of me. And makes them angry in the end. Or depressed.

"Come on, then."

He led me away from here, down and around corridors I planned to learn, to a door with no lettering. The whole place is like I imagine a brain to be, if you could live in it. Nothing in it too far from the rest.

This particular door was unlocked. There was nothing to steal here, that's why. Barring a few of those worn possessions which drop off a family as it jogs, never to be seen again, unless—like here—they've been saved. Two morocco-leather couches whose heads make a corner, all the torn places showing tan under the black. A piano. Some pillows much too silly to have lasted. In the jointure of the couches, where the telephone used to be and still was, a crocky brass lamp. At the foot of one of them, a crumpled old throw. I walked over to finger it. Said to be camel's hair once; by now it must be human skin. Its mottle was what memory is. Old on the eyeballs. The piano still said Kranich & Bach. Tackety-tock. Abe used to play a piece called Sentimental You on it, when he visited us. And the Continental Foxtrot.

"My corner," I said. "At 101."

"Abe's old office in Brooklyn, first. Then mine."

Not just 101 for me either; 101 was just the last. "I used to envy kids with houses—I didn't think you could save apartments."

Buddy laughed. "Saving is like spending, kid. A lifetime job." He sat down suddenly.

"Abe's office? How'd you come to bring it home?"

"I went bankrupt once and had no office. When you were just born."

I sat down on the other couch. Sentiment is any story you haven't been told. The more watery ones, usually. "Anything else I ought to know?"

"Why? I look sick or something?" He said it craftily, like they do. Wood-touching. Only his shoulders looked changed to me. Lost a little hope.

"Just saving. Like you said."

He fingered the phone. "She had an abortion the following year. After that, only misses. So you're the sole heir."

On the wall opposite me was one of my own brass-rubbings, sent him the winter before. I was already hung on a wall, a family artifact. Creepy. It was a start.

"What was she *doing* there, Bunt? In that glass thing?"

"Gambling. Signaling?"

"I went to college, too." His ugly style. And Abe's. "Fuck the psychology."

"In the dorm, we had two girls we were always breaking in on."

The men more often managed without signaling. Or with more success. Like yours, Betts. Or those are the friends I get.

"I should never have let her build that fool place."

That last little bubble from the bottoms? He couldn't mean it. He could.

"You couldn't help it. You're rich."

"That a putdown? From the ranks?"

"Sure is. Learned it from you."

I walked over to the piano to calm myself. Picked out a tune. Onka-bonka. Going to the front. Outside, the world is fair. "She said you give the parties now. You give that one?"

"I have a secretary, is all. Easier for Blum to send the invites. And then, if I want a few of my friends—" He stumbled. "I mean, like Leskel. Hard to separate business from pleasure these days. In our business." Then he did what they do, if we're handy. "It was your party, after all."

"She says she couldn't give the kind you wanted."

"So? I never wanted the parties, kid. Those parties. I'm a busy man. In a world she . . . Parties." He spat into the air. It was a good tycoon imitation.

That's where the stress is, onka-bonka. When you imitate.

"Not even in bed, she couldn't. She said." I saw the second capsule slip from his hand onto the Navajo rug Ike and I used to shoot immies on. "Tell you something, Buddy. Maybe it's only because I'm young. But I never yet paid for it."

What independence. Only one I have.

"Wait. Just you wait."

What else is fear?

"No it's not only that, kid. Look at yourself. You take after her. I'm the boy his mother had to tell him any boy doesn't look like a monkey is okay."

181

Eagle Eye

That's one way they get at you—humility. Do I pre-
fer pride?

"That lummox she had. A seed cataloguer. From
Idaho."

"Does she know you know?"

"I never said. In our family the women never—"
He shrugged. Put his head on his fists. "God, I have
to sleep."

Never said, never went downtown, never did. I
thought of the child I'd had for minutes—Jasmin's. I'd
have fed it all the music, from all the dixie cups.

He was scrabbling on the carpet for the capsule.
On the pattern I knew by heart, I saw it, in the cranny
where the smallest agates used to lodge.

He was watching me. "What do you think of us,
Quentin? Tell us the truth."

That trap.

"I mind inheriting it." My lips went stiff. "It'll come
on me, and I won't know how. Or even when. That's
the thing I mind."

"What will?"

"The shabbiness."

When he got up from the carpet, he studied the
piano, ran a nail so lightly over the full keyboard that
only one or two notes spoke. Came down hard forefinger, on middle C. "Shall I phone her? You didn't say."

When I didn't answer at once, he slapped a pillow.
Then the sofa. No dust flew, as it used to do. "I have
his number. I *talk* to him."

182

I picked up the capsule, still sticky from his hand. "I'd begin—not calling."

He lay down slow, white, his eyes ranging the ceiling. I could give him his pill. I owed him something. I searched the room, looking for it. "You sure one-upped me with this place, though. This room I mean. You sure one-upped me there."

Buddy looked at the wall. The computer-room, with its Zebel must be just outside, then the common room, the business ones and the pleasure ones, circled tight and interdisciplined, out to the city periphery that viewers up here owned.

"You don't mind about that, huh? You don't mind I one-upped you on that." He smiled.

"No, I like it," I said. "It makes me feel safe."

When he slept, I laid the throw over him and lay down on the other sofa, our heads almost touching. Before I had television in my room we listened to the radio like that. Or the record player. Falling asleep until Maeve called. One thing I had managed for him tonight. He got to sleep without that capsule.

I got up after a while and flushed it down the toilet. Toilet was handy here; food would come on carts down the corridor, as wanted; the girl-market would be as easy as dialing a prayer. And when she got here, no matter her size and shape for the night, that brilliant band of city windows would hem her in like a diamond-broker's inventory. Except for the room's having no windows itself, and a certain taint in the air of crushed apartments, it would be a handy place to live. I didn't suppose he'd figured in the computer that was just outside. I lay there, figuring it.

Now and then I could feel his breath on me, irregular. I could see how a letter to a son could be hard. Full of the naked family facts. So instead he wrote those crummy, humbly notes I got all year, full of his humility to my youth. Like the one I got in Paris that day and left on the washbasin, hoping the ink would run. He writes them virile, with a felt pen. "Full of his duty to me—what shit is that of mine?" I was holding onto Monica at the time, helping her over the bad spot. When she was coming down, she said, she always had trouble remembering who she was. She'd been repeating all the names she'd been christened with. "Monica Mary, shit. Isadora, shit." She croaked. "Wigglesworth, shit." She gave a hoot of laughter. "Ellsworth." She took a deep breath. "Shit. When all we want—." I wiped the spit from her hair. She was down. When she was leaving, she offered me her applecheek. The rest of her hadn't been much. "Thanks for the assist. Maybe it'll work out for me with those kids in Boston. If I can be an assist, to them."

He used to breathe over me like this, in my youth-bed. When I got a full-sized one, he stopped, and I was glad. I was king of the mountain then. They told me so daily. It made him angry now. When what I needed now was what Monica called, "the other thing."

I was on the same trip as her, really, I could smell

how it should have been. Never spelled out or pressed, but a birthright too. A sense of my duty—to them.

It's no trick at all to break away from a family. I can't understand the public concern. You can cut up a family in one day's night. With the facts. As a one-minute father, I knew that. But where do the facts go then? Can they be saved? Maybe there's a vocation in that.

I thought I heard the computer breathing, outside, telling me so. But it was only my father.

"Doughty," my father murmured, rolling deeper on his reef. "Blinded. They want permission to put *me* away."

"We sup with devils," I said.

In front of the computer it was cool as a field of cucumbers nobody had planted yet. I lay down on the rug with my face into the rug fibers, smelling the moths that never came.

I want to live in a room that is real.

What's smart about me? What's dumb?

◻

I went to see Janacek. Sitting behind a desk, he looks like a man with a lion's head over his shoulders. But you can see the seam where it stops.

"How is she?"

"Calm."

185

I doubted that. But it must be a relief to her that the sadness isn't joint anymore.

"Want to tell me where she is?"

"Better not."

He really believes we haven't guessed.

"Does she want to see me?"

"Rather not." He gazes at me without triumph. He must have to do this sort of thing all the time. For the families of the patients he is protecting from their families.

"She decide that?"

He nodded. I believed him. She's smarter than Buddy there. The Bunty-doll—she's throwing it away.

"Want to talk about it?" he said.

"You first. I'll watch your earring."

He laughed.

"Your mother was miming the stress put upon her," he said artistically. "Those weights."

"Screw that. It's a simple country device. Let the porch fall."

I could see her standing on the loaded back porch. Looking out. At the brambles.

"Amenia? Ah well, we believe in dwelling more on things that happen now."

"Me—I'm reading a book about time-binding." I was reading everything I could on that, and giving myself a course in the newest computer applications as well. And I was reading Babbidge at last. "You know we're the only animal does that? Binds itself to time? Even the king of beasts doesn't do that. Or so they say." I was watching his ear-wire, but it wasn't sending. "I'm not so sure though. Time's an audience. Haven't you watched even animals want that?"

"Animals?" He shrugged. "Animals."

I thought I could smell the camp on him. Far, far back in memory veins he no longer thought funneled that black blood to his heart.

"Sure, you know. Performing dogs. Horses at dressage." I mixed them more recklessly. "Flea circuses. Seals, kangaroos. Teddy bears."

The earring jumped. "Shall we talk about your mother, please? I have only this hour to spare."

He wanted to know. Already she was puzzling him.

He was formed to be puzzled if any child was. His own mother, sitting in her Queens kitchen all these years, folding gingham and ironing it, before the highest court. Jasmin went there once without his knowing. No gas in that kitchen. All electric. Very clean. No bones in the Disposall; it won't take them. But she was proud of it. When she died, he thought he had disposed of her.

"A lot boils down to what audience a person has. I been thinking that out. In front of a good one. Best I could find."

"God?" he said politely.

I burst out laughing.

"Ah. Another doctor, then."

I couldn't laugh twice. "A computer works by a magnitude of association, too. Only it isn't burdened with its own time sense. It doesn't have that dimension. For it, time isn't either a poison or an antidote. Time is only a test. And one life isn't long enough for all the storage it can take . . . Like if you could find a way to record your life in a 7090, you might have something. When you checked back."

He leans back. The better to observe me, he thinks. The resemblance is remarkable. Eyes used to seeing the kill brought in. The big cat's nose that must smell itself more than anything.

"A computer. Very chic. But will it listen? Like me now?"

We smile. At how much he must know about listening.

Everything—except that the children who talk to him nowadays are his audience.

"No. You'd be learning the language of your own life, that's all. In enough time."

If the computer could free us of our time—binding by seeing us free of it? By assessing us, assessing it all. As we went along.

I saw his fur stand up. But I wasn't afraid of him—yet.

"Like, we're so slow, Jannie. Like, when you told me about her—at my party. That second before you told it all. I was maybe a forty-five-second father. Or for minutes even. It gets longer and longer, in my mind. But it's too late."

"Bunty, we are not going to talk about her."

Aren't we. You are going to tell me about her. I am going to tell you about Maeve.

On the wall behind my head there was a picture. I saw it the minute I came in. I wonder if he kept the katipo.

"Want me to tell you about the picture behind my back, Jannie? . . . I will anyway. The shop also had one where the raindrop lines said *merde*. She thought that was too simple. The artist would do them to order, the shop said. But only if the artist liked the word suggested. And only five-letter words." There was one picture that said *other*, and one said *given*, but those two were bespoke. And one, the raindrops said *Deary*: she thought that was kind of nice—did I?" *Cooperative art, the village is full of it, though,* she said, and buried her head in my neck. "I asked her why she chose *nihil*." She bit me, and said did I know it was the Latin for nothing? "She said—'Because it goes with rain'."

We both glanced at the window. Today was rainy. She knew what she was doing.

"I always wondered, Jannie. If she ordered it."

He stared up at it, over my chair. I stared at my knuckles. People fall. In all variations. I suspect him of nothing. Except of knowing. "The day she was in that crowd was rainy. I looked it up."

I got up; in a second I was going to be very afraid of him. "Do you really believe? In light skulls?"

He lowered his head. I could smell his childhood

on him. It reached out for me. I stepped back just in time.

"Keep your dirty kid hands off that."

"I keep wondering if I should have broken in on her, that's all." I could have, once. He couldn't have. Too late for him, by then.

He knows that. She was wrong though, if she thought he doesn't feel. He's leading the linear life, that's all. They've straightened him out.

"I thought she always let you in," he said. Hoarse. When I came.

"I came to talk about her because she's dead. Don't we have to? Don't I? From now on, she's only in what we say. Forget I was one of her guys."

"Why are you here then?"

"What you said. Hunting necessity. I remembered it."

He was shivering like a cat about to spring. Forward. Or back.

"What we say of the dead—that's our language too, Jannie, isn't it? I never had anybody dead before. Much."

"Wait till you have hundreds. All the same age."

That whisper. How often she must have had to hear it, talking of the dead.

"The same age?"

"As yourself."

So that's why I came to him. *K-k-k.* Blood soy.

"I went to Riverside Church, once," I told him. "In that program they had—maybe they still do; why should it stop? Reading out the names of the war dead. You take your turn, then the next one does, like a marathon. After a while the names become a nothing. It's on a long roll of paper you hand to the next reader; you don't see the end of it." Then you go home.

He was listening.

It does help.

"I get a bug sometimes," I said. "Intestinal."

"All the deaths you didn't die," Jannie said.

"What do you do about it?"

"I wear an earring."

He got to his feet. "Time's up. Sorry."

Somebody ought to touch that seam of his. I wasn't afraid any more.

"Listen, Jannie," I said quick. "Watch out. About her audience. Maeve's. Buddy could take it small at home, because he had his business scope. But she never had a scope. So her audience stayed shapeless. And that's terrifying. That's why her white hair looks too old for her. She stayed young." How could I tell him quick enough? "She dwarfed the world down to him."

"Okay, Bunty . . . Okay, young man." He had opened the door. The next comer, a tyke, was standing there patiently. It sobered us both.

"I'm calling myself Quentin now. When you go home—tell her that."

He half-closed the door again. "*One* of her guys? You were the only one."

So that's why I came to him. To be told.

"I didn't pay in, did I Jannie? A machine would have done better. If properly set."

He doesn't answer. We've done our bit for each other, that's all. But I'm not his style of listener.

I opened the door to the tyke. Leaned down to him. "Touch his earring." And pushed him inside.

Small wars. Small wars.

But it'll be all right about Maeve. Jannie will talk to her like to a child. And she will cradle him.

◻

I went to see my father, who was in the kidney-machine.

Two of the cousins were just leaving him. One sister said loud in my right ear "Thank God—." The other, softly into my left one, "—that he can afford to pay for it."

We don't mention Maeve. Blum tried to get in touch with her. No soap, but Blum tried. The family is rallying round. All of us.

Because Buddy wants to talk about Maeve. And Buddy is going to be lost.

I talk to him about her, about everything. He's helpless now; even at his best he can't walk much, or screw, or work. And that—helps.

Watching him on the machine is like watching a

birth. Of a full-grown man. And during that time, all the time he can, he is watching me.

I do my best.

"Like it down there?" Buddy'll say. "At the office."

He's always a better color, afterwards. And he keeps a tanning lamp here. The only telltale is that over-clean look he has, of the well-hospitalized. In my mind I keep dressing him in street clothes, walking him down the corridor he does twice a day—and out. But the machine doesn't work on his heart. His faithful, imitative heart.

"It's neat down there. Great."

I'm living in that room at One Chase, weekends. And working up at MIT, on my life.

"Blum leaves me pies. Last week, apple. This week, coconut."

"When she makes it champagne, look out." He's got an imitation smile on him.

"I don't bring girls there. At least, not yet."

"Cambridge okay, hmm?"

"Cambridge okay."

"MIT's great, hmm; I always respected it."

"I'm learning to."

Doing a thesis on Babbidge, on what he might do with computers, if he lived now.

"Great stuff . . . Look behind my pillow. That section you gave me last week. I did it all."

At the start I gave him Babbidge, but he didn't dig it.

Digs everything modern I can get him; he's following my course. He'd be a hotshot at it, if he had the time.

Nowadays I give him all the pills he wants. "Not everybody in the class can do his homework on his own set-up."

"Works fine, huh? . . . I wish—"

Works like a dream, like a fucking dream . . . I wish he could.

"Lucky I only live there weekends. I'd never get away from it."

"David and Sol give you any more trouble?"

His loving partners. "Those two? Vultures in wolf's clothing. But at the moment, they don't have their eye on me."

"Who then?" His face went dark.

"Can they buy you out?"

"Ha. Not unless they persuade me."

"They're going to try."

"Ha."

"On the grounds you've got nobody in the firm coming after you. Or in the family."

"Nobody else but them, they mean."

Or me.

"Can you buy them out? Blum says the agreement between you and them at the outset was written so you always could.

"They can never get control. Even if we go public. I have the controlling shares. Plus the right to buy them

194

out at any time, at market value, plus a certain sum not less than their joint compensation. Based on their salary for that fiscal year—for the next five years. That was the deal."

I leaned back. Some men lean forward when they mean to make a deal, some back. I see it all the time at One Chase. Getting there a little early now and then, Friday afternoons maybe. Staying on Monday-Tuesday, a little late.

"Got the cash to do it?"

"Got the—." He chuckled.

I knew he did. Just doing everything I can.

"Then will you?"

"Who for?" It's been ravaging him.

I'm wearing a pair of shades I bought one Saturday night in Montmartre, because everybody seemed to be wearing them to keep their eyes from exploding in the fireworks of spring. Purple-green lenses (very popular that year with cyclists) that reminded me of the Jap beetles I had collected all one summer and kept in a jar on a window-ledge, until Doorman Shannon, spotting one, flicked the little mirror-back plague from my palm. "Want to murder the park?" he said. Sure enough, in Paris the next morning, the lenses turned out to be reflectors on their other side. So now, all that summer in Paris is an iridescent jar. And Buddy, looking at himself in my shades, sees a clean, little oval of a man, with plague.

"Saw Shannon the other day, remember him? The

doorman, at old 270 East. He's still working, two doors down." I'd passed him slowly but without stopping, thinking of causes and effects.

"Sure, Quent; I recall he had your same hair." Buddy knows in a deal you sometimes shoot out sideways; he's even savoring it. But he's short on time. "I asked you, Quent." He likes calling me that. "Who for?"

I leaned farther back. They had good armchairs in that hospital. To sustain the guests. "For me."

"Y—. But you just quit architecture."

He's afraid I'm a quitter. They always are.

"Money is architecture." A tour of his office taught me that.

"Builds houses, for sure." His eyes veiled themselves, before he reached for his own shades, black-lensed tortoise-shell. "But I've an idea you don't mean that."

"No."

"And MIT?"

"A computer is architecture. I'll teach it that." I leaned forward. "Other day, I finally looked up the word 'actuary.' Jesus." I pulled the dictionary page from my pocket. Like an eye that might explode. "One whose profession is to solve monetary problems depending on Interest and Probability, in connection with *life, fire, or other accidents.*" Italics mine.

"Insurance actuary? Like Abe? You want to go back to being that?"

I wondered if Abe'd ever written him letters. I put the page back in my pocket. If I ever had office stationery, I'd put that quote on it. If I ever had a son. "Why couldn't a computer handle *all* the probabilities?"

"What others are there?"

I could see them—for him. Memory and sadness, and the glass cage of family that had crashed from him, all joined together, keeping him alive and killing him, like a capon's breastbone sticking out of a man's throat. Even so, I whispered. "Why couldn't it help organize—a whole single life?"

He reached out and took off my shades. To see if I'm nuts. Or to make plain he thinks I must be. Any layman would say so at once. But he's had the course. And already he's reacting like the first man at MIT I spoke to. And the second, and the one those two brought in, a day after. He's already sold.

Just to say it, sells them. Just to hear it. "Can you implement?" they say, if they're on the inside—and start telling you how. Just to think it. The chance of seeing your whole life, in a clear eye-cup—it maddens us. Once it must have been like that when they listened to Freud.

"You could end up providing a service just like laundry," I said, not forgetting to laugh. A consultation service; organizing a man's knowledge of his own life." Not just for payrolls, or for interplanetary, either. For down here. And not just for crowds. You'd need whole banks of 7090's, or better. "It would be a life-bank like the records the government is building. Only every man

for himself." But all I'd need to begin is old Batface.
And me.

Experiment on yourself, that's in the tradition, the MIT
guy said. Pleased. *Data processing's a whole life for you
kids, isn't it. Anyway for a thesis, it will do.*

I was hoarse, and no wonder. I'd just written him
the hardest letter of my life.

"In exchange, I'll handle Dave and Sol for you,"
I said. "I'll learn the banking business, so's I can handle
them."

"Handling. That all it is to you."

"I *have* got ambition, Buddy. Just not the old ones.
Just—not yours."

We looked at each other.

That's all that's different. That's what's so sad.

"The hardest thing is still to tell, Buddy."

"Tell it."

"I want to bring in Maeve."

He leaned forward.

"I saw Janacek. He's not a man to stay with steady.
But he's very needy. So I don't know how long it will
take."

"Maeve down at the office again? You flatter
yourself." But he was still leaning.

"You'll see." I don't tell him I plan to bring her
in as a kind of partner eventually—the kind he would
never let her be. Maeve once studied to be a broker,
Blum said. I can just see her handling Sol and Dave.
Just hold yourself open for anything, I'll tell her. Like
people our age. You can do it. You did it once.

198

"Yes, I can see it," Buddy said. "It'll happen when I die." Suddenly he reached for my shades. Put his tortoise-shells on my nose. Put my shades on his.

I leaned forward. I saw blackly through his lenses. Behind mine, were his eyes exploding? It was a long time until spring. In the mirror-lenses, I saw myself, in him.

"Snap out of it," I said. "It's only a business deal. Abe *liked* Christian help, didn't he? For the humility."

The air in a hospital reverberates anyway—so why not?

"Won't you want to travel again soon?" he said, from behind. And from between his teeth.

"Nossuh." I could feel my old jauntiness rising between us. "I'll be a world-bum at home."

When I got up to leave, he was staring hopefully. I had brought him the right pill.

I wasn't at all sure Maeve would ever come back. But meanwhile it all helps, along with the kidney machine.

We are taking his wastes.

"Take it easy," I said, exchanging the shades. "You were brought up to expect the best, that's all. Us to expect the worst. It'll work out."

"Smart," he said. "Very smart."

Outside the room, I stood against a wall, exhausted. Love is obligation. You lean forward; you lean back.

A nurse came along. "What's the matter, kiddo?" When I raised my head, she said "Uh—ooooh ... Kid-do." Pretty girl, prepared to make something of it. When she saw I couldn't, she put a hand up, and patted. My shoulder. My cheek. Smiled. And went on her way.

Grace always breaks me up. Anybody's.

My tears for him sluiced through my fingers like his money. Nothing I could do for him either way. Live an imitation life, you get an imitation death.

◧

He went to see Father Melchior. These days, when he left the office, he went on foot—there was such wonderful chance in neighborhoods. The days were growing cold and he wore his jacket again for the first time. Souvenir of the hunting world his father had tried to put him in, it brought him back the guerrilla ways of summer. Ducking two trucks, he let a Yellow Cab tickle his heel, stopped it dead on his turf—he had the light with him—said, "Yalla?" to it as city boys used to do, and made it to the faded red-brick compound across the street, and up a set of those high Roman Catholic steps.

. . . This is the neighborhood Shannon once came from. Found him going on his lunch hour like always, for a sandwich and a snifter at his brother-in-law's bar. Shannon's father worked in a saloon on Ninth Avenue all his life. The brother-in-law's is still on Second Avenue, next door to a thrift shop. Used to be called Dugout For Buddies, now it's the Green Beret—that's how you missed it. Sure and I remember you boy, walk along. Getting to be hard, doing these ten blocks two ways every lunchtime; when I can't, I'll quit for good. Set 'em up, he said, when we were inside; here's one of my boys. Used to steal my quarters, he said, leering fondly. Sure an' it's Eagle Eye, I said, fellas, when the boy came up to me. The line at the bar laughed; they knew he didn't remember me. "He don't play that shill-game here." When they wanted to know where I'd been in the war, I said India. On reconnaissance. He's looking for a profession, Shannon said. Sanitation was still good, the bar-line said. Union tight as drum. But the Port Authority is still open. He's in with his father, you boobies. Shannon made eyes at them to let me ante for the beer after all. He's a *tenant,* Shannon said.

Even so, it's like standing on the beach, watching the worn glass roll in along with the stones; not many spars any more but lots of paper, and often it still says something readable, and just as you can bear to wrench your eyes away from that undertow, over there's a button someone wore last week or eighty years ago—and you tug it out—saved. Not yours, but related; nothing is lost.

Inside, the rectory feels like a trained audience. Hushed and respectful to all the sin and virtue that must come calling here. The old girl who led him into the empty study, telling him to wait, looked ready to clap for either side of it. Since he'd been summoned here, he couldn't tell her which.

The window here was decorated for the sea-

Eagle Eye

son—cut-outs and pumpkins, on 42nd Street! Bottom remains of Hell's Kitchen, still flowing with meat and fish and wholesale river air at the market end, working their way on up, from pimples-and-stilletto boys to that gun store just off Eighth Avenue, as it goes east. To the Main Library. And Bryant Park.

There were connections everywhere. He was finding them.

Coming out into the streets after a heady day at his console made him feel like an astronomer grounding himself, half-embarrassed at the purity of his work. Often it seemed to him that it was the computers who had the living-mindedness, and were only waiting to help the human mechanism free itself of the rote of history that held us back. He was no longer trying to record himself as the prime aim; that was the old post-uterine dream with which the psychiatrists had already grabbed off half a century. Process was the reality. No telling when—improvising one day at his keyboard—he might find another one.

He still went regularly to Cambridge, for workouts with "the boys"—as they called themselves—a group of men who had broken off from the university to form an agency for private projects, some as far-out as his, which they had housed in a ramped Bauhaus cube bought from one of the data-processors who had boomed and gone bust on Route 128. Weekdays, his hours in the office kept him from getting too rarified. Sometimes, with a weekend coming up, and when he felt his third-person sense of himself had honed itself down to the dangerline, he would give them a call: "Tell your boss, Bronstein says schizophrenia lurks—and how are *you,* Miss Cathcart?"—and whoever wanted a New York blow-out would fly down, bringing along any new material that interested them. Since he had put in a second console, more often, they sent somebody down on their own,—like kids to the boy with the most Tinker Toys. Salesmen of the infinite, he termed them privately—or in that daily-recorded realm which had once been private. Some had Radcliffe wives they were true to in the sack as well as the head; others wanted him to help them attack Sex City, in the bearded rock-style that was their Rotary. His celibacy of the moment didn't frighten him. They were all ten years older than he. And though he was trying them out, one by one, no crony had as yet occurred; perhaps he was too old for it. Or they were too eager-beaver for him, on the commercial side of their own marvels. Since his last ploy with Buddy, he had been avoiding that. Though he knew as well as they, that every time pure science had stuck a real needle in the infinite, money for somebody had streamed out.

Sometimes, fantasy had them sending him down a girl. Though they had girls on the staff, he had never asked; the scenario required that she be sent. Some Madame Curie-to-be, though not necessarily with him—to whom, after a hard day together sifting for a new language in all the modes of expression that weren't taken for granted any more, he could say "Allo, allo. Dos veedanya. Come close." All the intellectual girls

were gaudy beauties now, like from a new race of test-tube heroines. Meanwhile, Route 128 must now and then say what always would be said. "He's a rich boy."
.... Or did dos veedanya mean 'Good-bye'? ...

"Let me look at you," Melchior said deep. "I haven't seen you since." He turned me to the light. "You look fine."

He'd only seen me once. And I no longer stand for social talk. Like that language must be changed. If we're to find the other one. "Anybody's superior who's alive. Even a son. You can't help feeling it."

He has a great stone smile, like a natural phenomenon you can drive to see every Sunday, afterwards putting a sticker on the car to say you've been. Underneath though, is his hugeness different?—I only saw him once. He wears the smile like it's just given him.

First they send for you. Then they wait for you to talk.

"Thought priests had to be strictly on norm," I said. "Size and everything." Witkower's uncle hadn't made it because the joint of his little finger had been cut off.

Melchior's hand, the right one, perches on him like a rabbit, undisturbed by his chuckles. "In Friesland, I *am* normal."

"Friesland. I always wanted to go there." No reindeer but sub-Arctic dreams of them, and an endless skin of sea, spring like a short, bright-green pain. And the seven-foot people, like the Houyhnhnms surely, with seven-foot spirits to match—what a way to dwarf the world. "My grandmother was born in the town where Jonathan Swift went to school."

"Ah-h—uh?"

Meaning—if he didn't know what I was talking about, all was still received in the name of the angels. And the burden was still on me, to speak up.

I am trying. To say what I think—daily. But it's much harder when someone is listening personally. Or worse—theologically.

"Hear your grandmother approves of Florida, wants to settle there."

That why I'm here?

"Not to worry. I'm taking care of it."

Near the end of the calendar year—Gran had written—until that date, she reminded me, I could still avoid capital gains on the sale of the flat if I bought her a house.

He raised his eyebrows. Three and a half inches, each of them. The change from ordinary scale was restful. If you had another face, Batface—should it be like this? Like a good ogre? Or a horse? "We were under the impression—that Mrs. Reeves—"

No, Batface. It shouldn't.

"Had the money?" Poor Reeves. I didn't want to incriminate her. "I could be wrong. But then—why would she be taking care of Gran?"

His mouth could look smaller. "We thought it was an exchange of gifts. Some of them—intangible."

"Oy."

"Beg pardon?"

"A Yiddish expletive. Mentioning the intangible brings out the Jew in me."

"For it or against!"

I blew out my breath. He was hunched forward. All his lines of force. Cathedrals of them. Pointed at my little hack heart. It does make one feel valuable. "That why I'm here?"

"They did write. Asking for news of your progress."

"They?"

"Mrs. Reeves is—taking instruction."

"From Gran?" I started to laugh. Feeling in my pocket for Gran's spidery witch-note. "Yeah, she has gits. Though I can't see Reeves as a kleptomaniac." At the Miami-Hilton especially.

"Par*don*." He gave it the German pronunciation.

I took out the folded note. "The note from her you gave me that day. Day I came back from Wales. I stuck it away. Just came across it this morning."

He put on square specs. " 'Taffy was a Welshman.' " That was all. He handed it back. "What does that mean?" "A nursery rhyme. The next line is 'Taffy was a thief.' When I was a kid. I stole a couple of old silver spoons from her. To give to Maeve."

The specs slid forward. "Mrs. Reeves has been taking instruction from me." He took the slip from me and tore it up.

"Thanks. That was kind."

"Kind?"

"To both of us . . . Is that religious objectivity?"

"I mean the *word*, Mr. Bronstein. I hear it at the seminary all the time. Among the younger ones."

"Instead of 'good', you mean?"

He nodded. "When an English says 'That's kind', he used to mean only 'That's nice'. But now—"

"It's got its emotion back?"

He likes to nod, and wait.

Interlocutary conversion. Two can play at it.

Couldn't smile at his smile though. Like dropping a pebble into Melchior's Gap. So I put my head down to what I remember. The truth sticks there. "It's a word comes to mind when you think of animals."

He asked me to repeat: I spoke too low.

"Like Gran stinks as a person. But think of her as a cat—she's a howl."

He rubbed his hands. "*That* is religious objectivity." Rang a bell at his side. "Tea or coffee, eh? If we are going to have a dialogue."

"Two people don't have a dialogue. What they pick to say is only a millionth of what they could."

"I heard you were studying those machines. Thinking ones. Do they do it better?"

"In terms of multiples. But they have to be fed by people."

He laughed aloud. "And are you kind to them?"

"The best dialogue is between a p-person, and a—what you call a machine."

He stared at me. When the woman came in, he said, "Mrs. McMurter. Go down to the cellar and bring us each a bottle of wine."

We fell silent. I wondered what Friesland women were like. I smelled religion cooking. Or the creeping daily habit of it, that was set to rise like dough in the back of a bake shop, and ended every morning in a yeastly bread-image of God. "The house listens for you, doesn't it? Even when you don't understand things."

"The church does."

When the woman brought the tray, he set out the glasses, put biscuits and cheese to one side of each of us, in equal portions, like a referee, then opened the bottles—drawing each cork as smooth as I ever saw it done—and set the bottles center field table and opposite each other, like guns.

"Rhine wine," I said. "For dueling."

Then it struck me. He was being kind to me.

I let him pour. Then I took out the four joints I still had from El Paradiso, wrapped in foil in an old Schimmelpfennig tin. I'd known they were there all the time. But they were for safari. I held them out. "I drink your wine. You smoke my smoke." That sounded Indian to me. Hop-hop, into the war dance.

He lumbered to the sliding door, rolled it shut, and listened. Like a turnkey, but shutting in himself. On

42nd Street, whose rumble I could still faintly hear. The ways people can shut themselves up, and still think themselves out in the street with the common man, always interest me. As if I've always known I was going to have to do some of that myself. Libraries, study halls. Seminaries. Offices. And all the time, the common man is doing the same thing.

"I knew a man shut himself up in a tennis club. Winters. Came into Boston once a week to give our school indoor lessons. And to play bridge with his wife."

He sat down opposite me. "You've already had such a lot of experience. Worldly experience."

"What's the Christian for 'Oy'?"

His laugh was enormous. "You're a card."

"That was last month." But I could feel the talent coming back in me like a jaunty flower, up from the windpipe to the head again, with lesser branches for the ears. "You have to listen, to be a card." To friends. Though it doesn't look like it. "Where'd you learn that word?"

"We have a few, here."

"This the seminary?"

"The building in back."

I reached out and touched the joint he was holding. "Keep it for later, if you want—that's okay."

I could see the little carbuncle of greed near his eye. Better than he could see the hungry quiver at the back of my nose?

"Each to his own gormay? Why not?"

So it ended up he drank his wine, I smoked my smoke. Both of us listening. Let him think it was like in church; to me it was Indian. Once, I used to count up the cronies, like I never did with the girls. Now I did it again, in a sort of wood-touching. Ike, Witkower. Emilio from Siena. Betts. I couldn't quite add Melchior. But he had a face like a good ogre. Or a seven-foot horse.

I slipped on my shades.

"Take it easy," Melchior said. "I'm just a machine."

"Yeah. But I can see the building at the back."

He sipped, easy. "We don't shanghai."

"You been a sailor?"

"Padre on a troopship."

"Which war?"

He spread his hands. "Africa."

We tippled on. When I coughed once; he didn't laugh. Really I was trembling, with what I had to say to him.

"Nice jacket you have. Had one like it in the Congo once."

"Buddy got it, at Hunting World. Has as many pockets as a head. Haven't worn it since I got back."

"Where from?"

"London, Paris, the Low Countries. India. Wales."

"Odd itinerary."

"Yeah." India sticks out.

"How did you come to do it?"

"Deferment," I said. "How did you get to the Congo?"

"My mother was Belgian. She brought me up in her country. Where I was *not* normal." His grin was huge. Fixed. He put wine in it.

"Orphan?"

"I had a mother."

"Oh." A bastard. "Thought that was a blemish too."

"Par*don*?"

"Thought a—." The joint wasn't getting anywhere. "—bastard couldn't go for priest."

He put his big rabbit-hand on the table, as if might get away.

"Sorry. Hard to rap, when there's no frame of reference."

"Rap?"

"Dialogue."

"On the contrary. Only now I am the person. You are the machine."

"Ask me a question then," I said.

He took the cigarette from my fingers, sniffed it, put it down on the ashtray. I took his wine glass and set it away from him.

He squinted at me sideways. As if I were his wine glass now. Came close enough to peer into my shades, like an oculist. Raised one finger, wiggling at his image there. "What are the stations of the Cross?"

I jumped back. "Jesus."

He giggled. "The Jewish for Christ?"

I was meanwhile feeling something hard against my lower back, between me and the chair. The Inquisition, maybe. "How's Archie, by the way? He going to be the black for it?"

"Poor Archie's left us." He giggled again.

"For Ireland?"

"Because of it. Still a lot of patriots in the parish here, sons and grandsons of the old Hell's Kitcheners. He said they were too militant."

"You seven-footers, have to watch yourselves, huh. He go back to the game?"

"No, the Congo. Something wrong with that chair?"

I was rubbing like a cat for the pleasure of it, against an object in the jacket somewhere, whose shape I could almost define.

"Ants in the pants? Archie had them too. I told him what the abbot said to me when I was his age. 'Son, you belong better in the order of St. Benedict.' 'What's that order?' I said—'I never heard of it.' Archie neither. So I told him what the abbot told me. 'The order of St. Benedict, Melchior. Two heads on one pillow'."

"Find plenty in the Congo."

"I was already a padre," he said.

The drink was gone, the joints burnt to ash. We hunched over the table, both of us on the mark. Nobody said go.

I saw how his hand could be like my stutter, a tic from deep down, made public. Only, most tics mimed grotesquely or even sang, blurting up the life denied.

His hand sat on display, like the photos of themselves some savages hang around the neck as happy tokens from the other world. Had it always under his eye—this heavy hare that his God had made of him.

"Wooden pillows, they have out there," I said. "No, that's Japan."

The jacket is short on me. The object in its lining could be the reed flute that I bought from a blind boy in the plane stop at Karachi. Or it could be the joss stick I picked up at Bett's grave. I knew it was neither of them.

"Archie means to work for peace as well. Mind if I say something, Mr. Bronstein?"

"Do." I stood up, shaking out the jacket.

"You are a gentle generation."

"Not fit for this world, you mean."

"Fit to conquer it. The only ones who ever will."

"Ah, come on."

Back of the band for bullet-clips, behind the flask-pocket, and the patented waterproof oilskin ones for matches and holster—in case of rhino—there was a seam for a drawstring I never used, running all around the garment to its other side, where the slits were for passport, letters of identification and money-clip—and a note-pad, erasable with steel stylus, for taking bush-notes. I pulled the drawstring, shook the coat hard, and my knife fell out of it. Along with a forgotten stash of flat money, and a couple of postcards.

"Thought I'd lost it. It's called The Bush Wife."

No matter what the salesman called it. I waggled

some of its parts, with love for their domestic cunning, from the sliderule-and-level, file and burning-glass division, to the two blades—one to filet fish, the other to eat it with. I flipped it suddenly. Out sprang the nearest single answer to a switchblade. 'What's that?' Buddy'd said to the salesman. He'd looked us straight in the face. For wild boar. 'What's *that* for, the girls ask. Harakiri, the brave boy replies.

I held it out to Melchior, blade up. "Instructions? Give or get."

"Made a lot of converts in my time. For and against."

So it was an impasse. And the joint wouldn't take.

I don't know how long it was before I began to hear what the house was saying. Or he began to listen, in a way that let me feed him the questions I could answer. And let him answer the house. As if the wine in him was rising in me. And what I'd smoked, was wafting him.

"What's it like? To be an heir?"

"I've the kind of family won't disappear."

"I'd have liked a family," he said.

"All the deaths we didn't die—" I said "That would be a family."

And the lives we didn't live? He didn't ask it. But I heard.

Outside, the street gave a loud whine. Stretching itself, to get in here? Not a chance.

"Near the end of the calendar year," I said, "the pity everybody has for everybody has grown to the size of a pumpkin. You hollow out yours, cut a mouth of

214

teeth in it, and burn a candle in its head for all their souls. Around Christmas-time, you can usually get rid of it."

I was never able to.

Or did he say that?

Across the table, I saw what was wrong with him. "You're in mufti," I said. "Oh, poor man."

It was an old suit, European surely, too cheap ever to have been a good brown, too greenish now to be a good black.

"Indeed, I have no money. I've been spoiled. That's what they call a spoiled priest." But his smile was almost his own when he bent down to himself. "I leave, Saturday."

"Leaving here, you mean—or—"

He wouldn't look up. "Or."

That why I'm here?

"Need a place to stay?" I said.

"I shall be staying with a friend's. With a friend's relatives, that is, a brother. Until my job starts. And until she can take her vows."

"The veil?"

"Oh, no. No, no." That hand of his crossed to the other and clasped it. "She and I won't have much . . . apparently. I'm not a practical man. But we shall manage."

"Where's your job to be?"

"At the Museum of Modern Art. As a guard. Not my field, of course."

"Scarcely."

"Modern, I mean." He burst out laughing.

I remembered St. Sauveur. "No."

He fondled one of the empty bottles. "This seminary has a wicked cellar. Deeded from a parishioner who had a restaurant. Thought this was to be my last bottle of it. But I shall follow your thieving example and bring up one more. For a certain occasion."

We looked at each other like cronies.

"You're a card." I stood up, pocketing the debris that had fallen onto the table from my jacket—money, postcards. All except the knife, which I held out to him. "Thirty-nine uses, it has. You may find more." I couldn't offer him money; I could only do that if I was poor. "What was the name of that restaurant man by the way?"

"Why I don't know, son. He deeded it around your prohibition time. Why?"

"Had an R.C. friend whose father was going to have a restaurant. You never know."

He took the knife, careful of the blade. "Instructions?"

"A wedding present. Keep it for the road."

I showed him how every part fitted, and how to retract the blade.

"Thirty-nine uses. Can you spare it?" He was already in love with it.

"I'll remember I had it once. And that it wasn't lost."

At the door, Mrs. McMurter peeped. "Another call, sir. Will wait."

I was trembling. "If I once had a knife with thirty-nine uses, I ought to be able to remember how many ways people can be lost."

He'd found the burning-glass, and the compass next to it.

"Never very accurate," I said. "But can I ask you something?" I had come for it. "Don't we have to watch out for them? Keep track of them? L-like, aren't all the deaths ours? In any world I would want to live in, they would be . . . And isn't that the stations of the Cross?"

He took his time putting the knife away. One pocket he tried had a hole. "You're either a saint, Bronstein—or a Catholic."

Under the woman's eyes, peeping again, he blessed me. "Can't stop me, until Saturday." The big smile came back on him. "The disgrace to them; they're being very kind."

I saw he was prepared to be happy, in the sad, conclusive way of those getting ready to be joined.

He shook my hand. "Anything I can ever."

I thought of asking him about the women in Friesland, but killed it. "Thanks for the instruction. Thanks for everything."

"Thank *you* for it," he said, still pumping my hand. "That's why I asked you here."

"Me?" If he was thanking me for Reeves, he needn't. Limpets who never pry loose, who are never lost; there are those too; she was one of them.

Eagle Eye

"It was in my head before you said it, Bronstein; that I won't deny. But when you said it—somehow, that was the day."

"Said what?"

He walked me outside the house door and closed it. "Don't you remember? You said '*Mister* Melchior.'"

We were standing at the head of the high stone steps. What he had just said seemed improbably delicate for Forty-Second Street. I couldn't see the library. But I could see the gun store.

"Keep in touch, Bronstein. And remember now. Anything I—anything."

Last Sunday, at the Southport Sea Museum, what did I find but a piece of scrimshaw. With a lady etched on it instead of a whale. Even so, that the skinny-straight reality of those days came back to me. Another lost neighborhood.

"Ever run across anybody named Witkower, let me know."

"How'll I know him?"

"Catholic. They married him off at sixteen. He'll be around somewhere. In the suburbs."

At the bottom of the steps, I looked up. He was still standing there. He waved at me, like he was on a ship sailing for Saturday. I could see the hump the knife made in his pocket, that thin tweed.

But as I rounded the corner, the old jauntiness came over me. I could give him and Reeves the farm, why not? They might balk, but I'd manage it. If I'd already done what he said I had, I could do anything.

I made it back to the office in three skips and a jump. On my way, people stared into my purple glasses. I had lines of force.

□

Last night I went to the park, to try to be mugged. Over the winter, I've done that about once a month. It's always summer there. People without overcoats. Once I had my wallet taken, with a rabbit-punch and a snarl from behind, and thrown back empty of nothing but money, in front of me. "Freddie?" I said. "Freddie?" But whoever it was thudded away through the bushes. Once it was taken from me frontwards, all of it, with a black smile and a switchblade. "He's not Freddie, is he," I said to the black girl smiling at me. Her no-color friend said "Tell the man, no." And once a fag whose pass I mistook and held out my billfold to, squealed angrily, "I came to buy." Everybody's a veteran of something.

But now it's real summer again. And whoever hasn't frozen into a swan at the bottom of some lake, or died of beauty treatments at the Woman's House of Detention, might be coming out of hiding. Into a more natural setting. From whatever nest the winter has managed to knit for them.

This time I had a piece of Maeve's old loot with me, from the Michelangelo jewel box. That was innocent of me; I'm often that, still. But I'd learned something anyway. Maeve hadn't taken it with her. The bad-luck piece.

I was walking along the gray dusk in the mugging-hour, which comes later now, smelling beautiful. Having just checked the pavilion where the chess-players will soon come up as if planted and watered. Laughing at myself for my fidelity. The same paving-stone as last year can make me feel happy. Like adding to a jewel box.

On the public patio there's a guy sits. Wearing army issue. That could be anybody. That could be me. But this one's Spanish; he could be a Chicano. One of those desert-simple Diego Rivera faces, altogether with itself, like a bird. I try to see the girl Dina with it. When I come nearer, he says, "Watcha out the dogga sheet." He's got a weapon somewhere; I can see him shivering for it.

When I looked up again, there it was—a gun. Nothing from the armory room. Even sitting, his short legs were bowed around an invisible burro. Because I'm tall, he was pointing the gun up. A gun muzzle is like an anus. With a loose sphincter muscle. "Felipe—"I whispered. *"Esta tu?"* I don't know Spanish. I made it up. He frisked me, taking only the two tens he found where they should be; he too was a hander-back. "Other side," I said. "Little pocket." Slit they never see unless it's fingered for them. "There's twenty more." This is the moment it's dangerous, when they think I'm tricking them. Sometimes I put only ten there, sometimes a fistful

220

more. Not to be Robin Hood. Just to test what trust is left in people. My guess is Robin Hood never died of old age. So far I been lucky; maybe they can tell I'm aimless about money. Like them.

He was a truster. But Maeve's pin puzzled him. "You steala?" When I nodded yes, he made a kind of pal high-sign, shrugging a sorry. Carefully. I couldn't have taken the gun off him. Training it at me as he pulled away, he called back. "Juan. No Felipe."

I love walking back to my office home at night. Now that I'm about to leave it, what a Hotel Universe—its lights rising floor by floor with the cleaning women, or steadfastly wasteful, while the dark streets below coddle themselves inside their own arrangements, as bodies do when unvisited. By other bodies. And the solitary passenger hears the sonic dialtone of his only audience. On the way to the Federal Reserve the flash stores speak in vain, like deaf-mutes. Only I could see myself going down the block from one store window to the other—this odd, myopically interrupted frieze of oneself, little shadow that goes in and out with the city child, and will companion him all his life.

"Bunty," I said to it. "How now?"

The elevator tickled my flesh like a tease, and dropped me. I skipped from it, lamblike. Doing a hoedown. Going to Berkeley, onka-bonka, with a passel on my back.

Blum was still there at the fancy sink in her own cubicle. Setting her hair. An old habit she won't discard.

221

He paid her like a family man but kept her a subordinate. Since Buddy died, she's let the hair go from blond to gray—a task thing for a girl of only forty-five. "Mourning," she said coldly, when I asked her why. We held hands for two minutes. Then she blew her nose. "And so Push & Shove won't think I'm after the boss." The partners. She began calling me "the boss" to them right away. Buddy left her a stockholder. Between the two of us, and with me learning the business in the daytime, we have stood the vultures off. It wasn't the money. So much about money wasn't.

"Sign that stuff on my desk where it's marked, will you? The apartment closing is tomorrow." She packed her mouth with pins. "And bring tea."

Sold at a loss, to a labor-lawyer with a very large following. Whose wife likes to entertain lords.

"We made you do it all, Blum, didn't we?" Nobody ever went back. From the Miami Hilton, or the hospital. Or from the addresses, got by a chicanery Blum won't reveal, to which each month a check for Maeve makes a pilgrimage. There and back.

"I'm taking what I can. The paintings come here. That's very chic now."

She has a co-op in Riverdale. Gold and gunmetal, fur and glass, drapes lilypadding the floor, comfort to the breaking-point. Art would upset it. And men. The ones she has never stack up to Buddy. So she never lets them stay. Buddy was buried from it.

I flipped up the lid of the Michelangelo box and

put the opal back, on top of all the rest. "Take this too, all of it. Maeve never wanted it."

"Don't be sil. I'll bring it to the bank."

Maeve and Janacek are revisiting the death-camps, one by one. A pilgrimage, to dwarf the world.

"Some scientists found the edge of the world," I said. "It was in the paper this morning."

I went to my room for the tea, and backed out. "No, they didn't—" I shouted. "Everything on the other side of it's in here." Pinnacles and barnacles. A church shrine of piebald marble, loudly ticketed, "Miami." Where I had to admit it would look good. What appeared to be the contents of the armory-room. And five fur coats.

"Everything's going to storage. Had to get it out. You can stand it, for one night."

"Leave a coat," I said. "The white one."

When I brought her the tea, she turned off the hairdryer. "Had a girl here one night, didn't you."

"Right." A telephone contact. I paid for it.

"That's nice."

"No. Just didn't want to turn into an axe-murderer."

"Berkeley's informal." Her hair was dry already. "Want my nephew's address? He runs a sandal shop."

"Sure."

She wrote it down for me. "That advanced-study place you're going to. All graybeards, hah?"

"Not necessarily."

"All boy-geniuses, then." She had put the Wall Street

Eagle Eye

Journal clip on her bulletin board. All of them here
had, even Push & Shove. I hadn't done much yet except
have an idea. But the ideas of universal life-records,
yours and not the FBI's, could be a catchy one—from
the response to the story leaked from the boys on Route
128. Though I hadn't gone up there since, I hadn't
bothered to sever the connection. Understanding that
my itch wasn't too far from theirs. Good business always
has a life-basis in it, even in reverse: dentures, deodor-
ants, headaches. A computer-dating-process with your
own mind—as they called it—might fit in somewhere
in that melancholy line of prostheses for going on. But
the Journal had picked up a personal angle—that I was
taking my own equipment along with me. "Like a typew-
riter—" I said to the interviewer "—that's all." I've gotten
used to it. It's a common occurence in computer labs;
check IBM if you don't believe me. The cling between
a data-processor and his pet console gets very strong.
"Mebbe so," the man said. "But then, there's the way
you're taking it. Along."

If I'd just shipped Batface west—done all the time,
the air-cargo people said. But I was going with it, in
the freight plane. Like men used to do with bodies,
in the boxcar. Or with dogs they loved. "I just wanted
to fly a freight again. In Europe, there were groups
of us did it regular." The reporter was a guy from Brown,
not much older than me. "Going west, young man,"
he muttered, penciling. "That's still a story in America,
would you believe it?" *Boy genius goes West*. I looked over
Blum's shoulder at the lower heading. Rich boy.

"Girl geniuses too, maybe." I watched her sadly. I'm a sucker for any woman at a sink. "Maybe even robots."

"Send me one."

"Yeah, I will." Penguin-shaped. Answers to name of Buddy.

The limousine rang for her from downstairs. She gets the partner treatment now. And still checks the desk, windows, lights—like a secretary. She saw me see. "My outfit I have on cost seventeen-hundred dollars. But I still feel guilty a two-hour lunch."

"You have to be aimless with it." I gave her a hug. "Bye, Blum darling."

"Why do you have to go?"

Why do I?

"Just want to spend a little time in the suburbs."

"Bye, Bunty." She never fell for Quentin.

"Hold the fort."

"You coming back, then?"

"Just a phrase." That you say to a Blum. She knows that.

"The werewolf of Wall Street." I gave her a kiss, socking it.

She pushed me back, hard. "You just have no contempt for women, that's all. Maybe for anybody—I've been watching you. Just put up some barbed-wire, will you, Bunty? You need it." She left quick.

It's too late for that. The rich can be hemmed in just like other people.

I went to the window. Where insights abound, for

all those bred to the charms of height. Financial clerks, and other mountain-climbers. Sunset aficionados, on the fire-escape. And even porch-standers, one step above the blackberry-bramble bush. Newsboy philanthropists doing their leather-couch dreaming—with one foot a Montefiore, the other a Rothschild. Soldier-prisoners, imprisoned from the start, stepping alive or dead out of the homing bombers, into the actuarial light.

Lights of the World, Edges of the World, Eagle Eye surveys you.

How greedy I was. I still treasured and mulled over all the people who ever shared my landscape. How else could any one of us be sure we were each one wanted—it had to do with that. "When the leaves turn," that girl Dina had said "Maybe I'll be back for mink." I liked to hear that, in its lonely corner in my mind.

It meant a continuity, however shabby. It meant a kind of life-by-association, however guilty. It reassured me that even my mother, in her shady role of providing coats and abandoning them, would continue to be there. I want to keep them all. All the shabby people. Every one.

To do it I would have to be there to people more than I had; I would have to pay in. Obviously I couldn't do that to all the possibles in my past, or in the mists to come. It would be more like standing on a street corner, talking very hard to someone, or to a chosen few. As the real one, or the one lost, came up or bumped into us. That way I could be present and open to the chance of all the others. I could be waiting to be found.

Sunset like a line of sludge-water. Indian file of palisades gone pop. And a bale of sky-fog over all. But still there it is as we were taught it, the Demeter-diameter, the radius of the earth, straight or curved.

Why dwarf the world at all?

Then it came to me that I might be one of the ones who were lost. For the first time I thought of myself as one of those. To what others, over there across the thin dividing line that keeps a memory from standing before us in the flesh, am I one of the lost ones—to them?

I was that to Jasmin. To her I am irretrievably lost.

From now on, to be here, I'll have to bare my breast, teeth, and tongue, even louder. So as to be sure. To be found.

Night came, the sunset was gone, but surely some photographer would have saved it, or some retina. Maybe his own. He went into the kitchen and rousted himself a short meal from one of the refrigerators. There were three of them, witness to the levels here. He took a sandwich from the coffee shop one, a chicken salad from the one that furnished for the executive dining room, cut a slice from the molded Beef Wellington kept in reserve for distinguished guests at the director's table —and laughed at himself for the quickness of his rise. A meteoric career. He left a few traces of himself for the morning Helgas—they too liked to know who they served—then darted into his packed room, and stood there bemused. The shrine had tilted a little with the evening. As religions did, maybe. There was no statue in it, maybe never had been. An arcade for lovers was more its air. He lit the light under its arch, more for it than for himself, then went out the back door of the office, giving a pat to old Batface on the way, as to the family animal. It was that. But not a dog.

□

The barman of the Lotos looked up as he came in; so did the other men there. The bar had moved on a few blocks, but no one could say where; he'd had to find it himself. The streets along here sweated urine, spilt milk, mucus and fruit-skins, but no small talk. Each hallway passed showed a dim coffin-space. Now that he was on an errand he was wary, but nobody came at him. Maybe he looked as if he had a knife.

"Nobody move," the barman said. "I talk to him."

He saw himself in the mirror then, tall and flame-haired in this house of short-legged tawniness, and bearded black. With a woman's coat on his arm, but no woman.

"Easy does it," the barman said. "Don't want no trouble. Put that thing somewhere."

He looked down at himself. "I have no gun."

228

"Who said gun?" The barman touched the coat. Thick paw but deft. "Ain't that mink? Sure is. You been on Broadway?"

"Never getta that on Broadway. My wife, she was cutter." A man got up from one of the two tables, to look at the coat. Small, with a sombrero air to him, even in a shirt and boots. He could be a Chicano. Any of them could.

"I'll handle it. Don't you fellas see the time?" The barman opened a door to his left, pushed Bunty and coat inside, and closed the door.

He was in the can. Alone at last again with the familiar ruined porcelain-and-brown, he did his little dance of recognition, as all over the world. Pissed. Paused at the doorknob, as usual before company again—girls, journeys. Could almost think they'd expected him. Not the Messiah, surely. He hung the coat behind the door, and walked out.

"You should locka heem." Another voice, from behind.

"No." The barkeep shoved a beer at him, quick. "On me. Drink, will you."

As the policeman sauntered in, he repeated it, his eyes like ant-holes. "On me."

The cop's shrewd black gaze picked him out at once. The others in the bar went movie-tense. His own roving inner spotlight stayed cool. Somewhere far back of it, he felt united with them, as if he had seen that movie too.

"New here?"

He nodded. Once he opened his mouth, the syllables would fall out like money and save him. He wanted not to be.

"See your driver's license?"

"Came on foot."

"*License.*"

A point of law flicked by him—*habeus corpus?*

"Fifth Avenue. You work there—Quentin?"

A man sniggered.

The policeman turned. "Thassan English name." He swung around, taunting. "Ainit?" He had absolutely regular "white" features, un-negroid, un-national, beneath a blue-black skin. The effect was of two men, one inside the other. Neither of them relishing argument.

"I don't know."

"You dunno? Mine sain yo beerzness roun heah?"

"Looking for a friend."

"You come all the way up here, looking for a friend?"

"Never see him before, Seempson," the barman said. "Not since I have the place, six month. He just walk in."

"Yeah, I know, Dominguez. You run a family place. Uh-huh. Why I have to check here every night . . . Been overseas, Mr. Bronstein? . . . You have. Asia? . . . You have . . . Bring anything with you?"

230

He saw how evidence worked. The simple pace of it dazzled him.

"A little. Smoked the last of it yesterday."

"See your discharge, please."

"Don't have one."

"Don't you. Now why? Now, what do you have?"

He should have had nothing on him but the usual two tenspots, but he'd been to the bank for travel cash, and had also volunteered to buy a present for Blum's niece, since Blum had to be at the flat all day—and had forgotten to leave his wallet at the office. So he had $750 in cash, plus traveler's checks making it a thousand—the exact sum Buddy used to send him, kept now like a boundary between him and all the money available. Also in the wallet was his passport, airline ticket, old draft card. And a woman's charge-a-plate, marked Beatrix Blum.

"Told you. He rolled somebody." Dominguez was quivering with money-heat. They all were. It lay on the cop's palm, blossoming like a green bay tree. Or a shaggy green key, made of paper only. Key to his own jauntiness. Like those babes born on dope he'd seen having the bends on television. Born to the money-fix. Simpson's palm was trembling, too.

"I am a computer-programmer," he said quickly. Always brought them to attention. "I don't really know my name is English or American; I was named for Teddy Roosevelt's son got killed in the First World War. And for my father. I'm living in my father's office, temporarily. Because the apartment on the license there, that was sold. I never lived there but when I got a new license, I gave that address. My father died, a while back. My mother left before that. With somebody else."

He saw he had their ear; he was sorting out some of the same bald facts that went with their own Cézanne hats and cardplayer shakes. And sloe-eyed greed. Nothing has ever malformed without a reason. They knew theirs. "I go to California tomorrow, to learn more about the business; that's what the money's for. Bee Blum is the woman runs the office here. She was my father's girl." His voice ran out. "She was plain Beatrice, once." He mustn't smile. He could hear the terrible lesson he was teaching them, in his slim other-language. Of how things were, over the edge of the world. "A friend I had—they used to hang out here. I always meant to come by."

"When? I know every hombre my bar."

"Summer."

Dominguez let out a breath. "Not my time."

"I am customer from the old place." The man whose wife had been a cutter. "What your fren name?"

A sharp burst of Spanish from two men at the table. The man waved it back.

"*Manuel,*" the barman said.

Manuel ignored it. "You say?"

"D-Dina," he said.

"*Como?*"

He understood that. "A girl. She traveled with a guy named Freddie. Felipe."

The barman laughed, spoke in Spanish. The table leered back. Everybody relaxed.

"Freddie was sick," he said.

"Where?" Dominguez.

"In the bowels. From the war."

Manuel shook his head.

"I came with a present for her."

Dominguez translated. A great joke.

Manuel spoke in Spanish to them.

He understood it by the tone maybe, in his animal ear. Shut your mouth, mothers. This is a good boy.

The cop was still poking at his stuff. "Jesus, another student. It ain't enough they drive cabs." He addressed the two tables. "This couple he says he knows. Nobody ever heard of them?"

Nobody. It could be their stare was policy.

"This couple, what was their beerzness?" Simpson did have two accents. The man inside the skin dared him to notice it.

"They were living in the park."

No surprise.

"Girls sometime, the old place," Manuel said. "No here."

"Manuel the volunteer," the cop said.

"You like girls, why you here?" Dominguez washed the bar slowly. "No wives here, even."

"Hear that, Manuel?" Simpson said. "Well, *hasta la*

vista, boys. You Bronstein. Come on. Give you your stuff outside."

"Thanks. Think I'll finish my drink."

"Suit yourself." Simpson studied the passport, shook his head over it, handed it and wallet back. "Good night, Dominguez. Ah . . . my beat ends a coupla blocks on, Mr. Bronstein. Then I plan to cover back. Or maybe I just hang around outside. Got it, everybody?" He left.

"Have a drink with me, Mr. Manuel?"

"Gutierrez."

"Gutierrez. To the girls, Mr. Gutierrez." They drank. He blushed. Forgot something. "Bronstein."

"*Como?*"

"My name."

"Brawnstein." The two drinks they had could travel in a minute to those bowed receptacles, Manuel's legs. His boots shone firm. He drank Irish, worked for the police stable. "The mounties." He grinned. "Simpson, he want to go there." He wore a sharp white shirt. Like some horsemen, he looked cleaner than other people. "These girl—she pretty, hay, she New York?"

"Not New York." California? Lindenhurst?

"What color her hair?"

"Dark."

Now that he had hunted her in good faith, could she begin to disappear into his imagination? It wasn't her he hunted then; what was his necessity?

"Mebbe this Felipe, he die. I like such a girl. My wife die." He had a room on the hallway next door;

his sister had the kids. "Everstrow, up the river. Big Spanish there. Barrio."

"Haverstraw." Dominguez met Bronstein's eye, almost human, like a fish swimming past you underwater, side-eyed, intent on its own. But seeing you.

"This girl, she drink a little? Ah, *sí*. I like such a girl."

Manuel had taken her over. He could leave now. The possibility of her would be visited, from time to time. The human chain goggled at him. The beer pressed his bladder. He made for the can.

Dominguez side-stepped him. "Want something?"

"A leak."

"Out of order. Sorry."

Everybody at the two tables was watching him. The coat—he'd forgotten it. He mustn't smile. He should have bought a round for them, those cardplayers, but had been too shy. Now he couldn't. They stared dream-like. As if he was their dream.

"Suit yourself." He walked out.

Simpson stepped from a nearby doorway.

"Got everything that's yours?"

He considered. "Yop."

"Manuel still in there."

"By a hair."

"I better get him. Some night, he gonna get it." Simpson didn't move.

"Why?"

"Lotos was busted. Last summer."

"Going to be busted again, ha?"

"Working up to it."

"And Manuel won't buy."

"When the bust came, he was at the hospital, with his wife. He and she used to go in there every night. Can't turn him off the place. Six other Spanish bars, my beat. He won't go."

He took a moment to transfer his stuff from an outer pocket to an inner. For the morning. "Maybe he's waiting to be found. Don't knock it."

"You think he's buying?"

He considered. When they sold the coat, would Manuel take any? "No, he won't buy. But he'll go along with it."

"Not too far." Simpson rubbed his teeth. "Funny. They must know they'll be busted. But it's the kibitzer who'll make them sore; I've seen it before."

"That why you're following him?"

"Come again. He's teaching me horses. Puerto Rico, he used to handle them."

"He didn't really look like a Chicano. None of them."

"Why should they—Why'm I telling you this?"

"Because I don't drive a cab."

"Smartass. Maybe you better come down to the station-house. *Know* I seen you somewhere. Down at the hack-license bureau, maybe. Checking something there only today. Maybe you better."

For Blum to get him out in the morning. Or Push & Shove. "I'll miss my flight."

236

"More I look at you—flight, huh? Lemme see those papers back."

"Maybe you saw my picture, the Journal."

"Is no Journal, anymore."

"Wall Street."

He felt flattened suddenly, without a sound. Though he was still standing, the street came up in his eyes to remind him that this was what men walked on, here.

Simpson was looming over him. "You undercover, huh? You won't fine annathing. I'm straight."

"Your accent's come back," he said. "The other one. Maybe the shot was picked up by the other papers. It was in yesterday."

"The News, that's it. We get the News. I remember you. But I don't know who you were."

Who was he? It was like a charade. "I was the one going to take his computer to California."

"Jee-zuz. The fine-ancial genous. Sure 'nough." Simpson took him by the chin, ran a little screw of a flashlight over him, the dropped his hands as if he'd been in the till. Or touched too much money. "Sure 'nough." He broke suddenly and ran down the block to a trashbasket, pawing there. Funny. To see a policeman run. He never had.

"Here you are."

He saw his own picture the way a savage might— black lines, white space. "There I are."

"Got any tips on the market?"

237

"You play?"

"Sure." Simpson poked a finger in his ribs. "But I'm straight."

"You know what, you're a comedy cop. Acting like what you already are."

Simpson smiled. "Cain't all be genouses." He was bright as billboards, and knew it. "What's it like to be one of those anyway? C'mon, give."

He considered. "You can't see too much too young. It's un-American."

Simpson spun the flash over him again. "You on anything?"

"Not a thing."

"What you really come up here for?"

"A girl."

"Girl, huh. Yeah, you said that. Gimme it again. Name of?"

It came to him like a tip. From the weather man. "Jasmin," he said.

When he wouldn't say any more, Simpson hailed a cab, and told him to get the hell *hell* out of the neighborhood. Where should he tell the cabbie to go? "One Chase Manhattan Plaza, pal, and see that he gets there. He got the fare." He leaned in at the window. "Jesus. Why *don't* you just drive a cab."

When he paid off, at the curb, the cabbie himself was worried. "There's nobody here."

Then why worry? "It's all right. I know the night watchman here. Just going to say goodbye to him."

The cab drove off before he heard the oddness of his excuse. Should at least have said it was to say hello.

He passed the Dubuffet, which was still frogging it. Nobody here but us animals. The repetitions of the night had begun to get him, as in the worst dreams. But also, like the repetitive rhythms of his own body, which, chewing its way between excess and evenness, was only intent on telling him how to live with it. Maybe he was being taught the rhythms between life and dream—while he was awake and sane, and shivering.

Upstairs, he walked the periphery of the office. Ending up as always.

Well, old Batface, what's for winter? Don't tell me. The prospect from One Chase at night is pretty overwhelming still. That river, the dark towers of World Trade, the gaps of earth where the raw-siena oxide reminds any building here of its mortality. Or those one or two Revolutionary structures down there, which remind the country of its birth. Whose only dissidence now is that they are wood. Between them and me, an early-century Artemis, no longer gilded, or seen from below. Money is architecture is time...The clear clouds wait for the armistice still.

I could, you know. I could call up the stewardess. The last night in a place you have been always gets to you. No matter where. No matter if it's already dawn. And the van is expected, shortly, as all vans are. And early—all the long-distance moving on the planet must

begin at eight o'clock. The movers in the best arrangements bringing wrap-cloths of their own device. If necessary a sofa can be moved with a man on it. Or a bedpan
with three lightbulbs in it, and a pony-tail switch—there's
always a last minute little something extemporaneous
to mock all movings with, even the best.

Now I have a confession to make, Batface. Computers can be lied to, so easily. The lie I told you was
maybe a small one. Still I want to correct it. Maybe
because I am a man.

Long ago, long before I ever went world-dwarfing
in a big way, I did find Ike.

He had gone to Riverside Church, to serve his
time as one of the readers, who in continuous round-
the-clock succession, were reading aloud *in memoriam*,
from a list of the war dead, whose names were arriving
in continuous succession, from Vietnam. He'd been out
of high school a year and a half. As he walked through
the lower-office regions of this church that was half like
an office-building, to the little chapel-place where the
reading was being done, he understood the nature of
his protest exactly. He was against a rhythm of the world,
uselessly. Trying to weave his own bit of religion, in
a dark room. Others, it was true, had been before him
and would be after, in the same place. But when the
scroll was thrust into his hands and he stood before

the lectern—had there been dais, he couldn't recall?
—he was as alone as if he stood on the bract of a cloud,
up from his own grave, and heaven already behind him.
The scroll, about the width of an old pianola-roll, reeled
endlessly from his hands and mouth. Was it sacrilege,
to pay honor this way?—and why was it more honorable
to die than to be saved, to do this?

Ever so often, one of the hat-ladies from another
part of this eclectic church nosied in, sniffed out. When
his relief person didn't come, he was asked if he could
go on, and went on. He began to hear his own voice
as one of the details of the room, in among telephone
messages from those who could or couldn't come, and
the steady voice of the girl who was taking them. He
must have been five or more names past it, when he
heard what he had said. "Isaac Joseph Isaacson." Yes,
there had been a dais. He put the list on the lectern,
and stepped down. "It's all right," the girl said, smiling
at him "your relief is here. He was only waiting for
you; he didn't want to break in." And up there at the
lectern a tall basketball-thin black was already reeling
it out. "Funny, yesterday it was all middle-aged mamas,
today it's all guys," the girl said. "Can you come the
same hours next week?" He couldn't say—no thanks,
I got what I wanted. She had too nice a face. "S-sorry.
G-going abroad." There couldn't be another such
Isaacson, and there hadn't been—he had checked. The
following week, he had gone abroad, on a last-minute

two-week deal—he hadn't liked lying to that girl . . .

"Isaac Joseph Isaacson," he said aloud, now, "Trapped on the Meuse. Remember Verdun."

Be somebody, and they have to hunt you up.

He put his hand on the metal casing in front of him, watching his palmprint breathe there for an instant, then fade.

I want to keep them alive for a while, that's why I lied to you. Finding them isn't always the best.

He'd searched his jacket dozens of times for that one postcard she'd sent him, telling himself that it might still lurk somewhere in those seams. Thumbing through those that had. Sometimes he got up in the middle of night, recalling still another crevice—and looked again. But in the underpocket that lasted beneath all lies, the sentence on the card kept itself half safe for him. "How's the summer soldier?" it said.

He leaned his head against the console, that six-month companion-at-arms. It still had a voice, codeless except to him maybe, but no dream. Alas poor Yorick, is that you, Bronstein? Hang your head on my armor. Let us dwarf the world. O perfect fool.

Dozing against the machine, he spread his arms wide. The computer is the cow. In the steamy morning before the world wakes, I feed you. I lean my head against your flank. But you lied too, you know. You're not Betts.

Neither is he.

242

Excuse me, Betts. I beg you the deepest pardon of all—the one we exact of the dead. You know that you can be pushed aside.

Excuse me all.

EOF. END OF FILE

He woke from a dream of heights. He often thought of the console in front of him there as a window. And when standing at a window, of the console, he got up. Fenestrate, Bronstein, that's your kick.

As he was waiting there—for a sign like in the old folklore or a judgment of lightning to streak his sky—was that it?—he saw what at first he thought was a dog running down the street, only to circle the Plaza, and reappear. To see a dog run foaming down the street, from more than thirty stories up, and wonder whether it was a man really, and in the split-second after, know it was a man—what was wrong with his eyes?

First there was the image received on the retina, and then what the brain did with it. He could walk round this perimeter again, and test both. Inside him, he was afraid that at every view, north-south and south-west, he would see the dog-man, thirty stories down. There was no unobstructed view to the east; even Buddy's millions hadn't bought it all.

He decided to go downstairs. In the split-second before closing the door, he reached in again for his backpack, kept ready along with his keys. In the second after closing the door, he found he'd left the keys. In front of old Batface, like an offering. Down the elevator he went, one of his ears opening as it always did—down the stairs of his mind, meanwhile.

When he got outside, he saw what looked like a bundle, far down the edge of the plaza. He was afraid of visions, but went toward it, screwing up his eyes. The four-thirty dawn rose like a mechanism of pewter planes and cubist shadows. These days, did you have to see all the galleries to understand the physical world?

Dog or man, or even child, the bundle far down the street was still moving. It was what a soul on legs or a legless beggar-on-wheels might be, humped or curved, rolling about the world in rags or shadows, with morning light about to stream down on where the crown of the head should be—if that was a head, and illumine the chin with dusty human contours—if that was a chin. Souls ran along the streets like Easter-eggs or stones, in all guises.

When the clout came from behind him, he was ready. Everybody in the city was, of course, but this particular clout was for him. As he sank, running on a few steps with the blow, his jaw wide, his last thought was of someone thirty stories up, and looking down on him, wondering whether he was a dog or a man.

He woke to the smell of whales. Harbor-gut. He could almost see them though on the waterfront, in from

244

the Narrows on their way to the Kill Van Kull to be etched on ivory. Or beached and gaping, their jellied insides being visited by men in stovepipe hats. There was something very American about them—or about thinking that there was. Mother Russia, Uncle Sam—a dog-man was a citizen of more. Someone coming out of the coffee shop nudged him with a toe. He felt for his wallet—gone of course—he had been followed. He was down in the gutter, dirty, and not ashamed of it.

He felt for his stutter. His most intimate possession. For the moment he felt cleaned out. Time would have to tell whether he had lost it for good. Or another person. Takes two to stutter, doesn't it, Jasmin said in her teasing bed-voice. *Like tango-ing.* He got up from the curb, feeling his head. On the crown of it, a little cockscomb had risen, a thin ridge to the thumb, full of young tenderness. His ideals, maybe. Seemed as likely he would go back to the office now, as that he wouldn't. Rolling along the street in his soul-curve, he and the street would have to decide. As he limped along, he could see his early-morning self flitting from store window to window. The purple glasses were gone. His vision was 20–20 now, as the oculist had sworn it would be. He was Batface, had been all along. Bunty to Quentin, Batface to Eagle Eye, one plane ticket would carry them all. He was so hungry-healthy he could eat a whale now, imagine it later.

But down-under and blocks away, the Flying Tiger

van must already be rolling onto its platform. Might already be loading, the crew of three gone upstairs with their dolly and embalming-cloths, the driver sitting in the cab, a two-sided metal-man, faithful as a toy. He knew van-handlers; how they liked to be finished at three, home with the feet up to a beer, in a house or a garden often described—hernia at fifty, arthritis at sixty, but afternoons free. How any man might need to make his life visible in the most ordinary way, to allow for the unearthly that must creep in.

In the theatre of the invisible—Buddy now said to him—there is never any want of space.

He stopped in his tracks. Not to hurry, kid. In part, you are now what the dead make *you* say.

The long van had already loaded. Traveling like a behemoth with its mouth open, it had snapped up this last cud. He peered in, and saw it, shrouded. Nobody sick in the back. A good outfit, the Flying Tiger of Newark. He'd chosen it out of the phone book, second try after Cherokee, which had turned out to be more of an airline. Knowing plain enough why the Indian name called to him; why animals kept floating into his head, he couldn't say. Two by two or alone, taking up what appeared to be their accustomed places. Or else in silent congress, paws uplifted, leaving him to make the analogy. Maybe it was because they were out of time. Or were his luck.

He heard the crew grumbling at the wait. Boss must

be soft in the head—a passenger. What kind of freight was that?

One of the crew rubbed two fingers against a thumb, under the speaker's nose.

No, he'd booked at a price, but without bribes. That had been attended to long since.

He went up to the crew. "Waiting for somebody?" Van-men would talk to anybody except the people in the house they were moving from.

"Yeah, some wook, has to go along with this bundle."

"A wook?"

Whether they were hewn and musclebound, or shaky non-unioners off the vino for the day, he always felt secretly allied. Shaggy wagoneers, blunt-headed shunters of space, their heavily mantled shoulders sloping to hindquarters where the rut and the dance was, buffalo.

"He means a wack," one of them said.

"No, he doesn't," a second one said, "he means a kook."

They all three grinned at him.

"That's me, I guess. The name is Bronstein."

They scanned him.

"Musta weighed him double."

"Use him for a tail pipe."

"Pop him out of the top, like for a Diesel."

They put him in the cab.

He was glad of it. The vitality of his adventure might

surpass anybody's here, but he didn't want to go it alone. The Bronsteins were moving again; it was his heritage. Though it was the ports that bothered him, he would settle for the journeys. Abe's coin had paid for this one, long time a-coming.

Maybe I'm a pioneer, like Babbidge. Maybe I'm a failure, like Betts.

"Where you going, kid?"

"C-California."

What's for winter? Summer.

He saw it ahead, beyond Newark, a land of golden roses stiffened to bronze, a tale not quite despised. No one can be a soldier all the time. Not even a soldier. Now and then, I'll call you all up.

"What you got with you?"

Wrapped like a coffin, or a bomb. Or a birthday-box.

"A p-piano."

He had his stutter back.

As he skittered along, it sang. The jangle of personality that everybody was, rode along with him—a tinkle of manacle at the wrist, a chain-gang at the anklebone. The song of the first loss, training him. What are we here for, here for, if not to see each others' lines of force? And see them, see them pitiful. Bunty stood and smiled, and kidded. Quentin beat against doors, and performed. Eagle Eye saw. The postmistresses of Ireland and Wales shook hands-across-the-sea with him. Wander the life-camps of the world, oh freely deferred. Oh per-

248

fect fool, you are at the beginning of life. Somewhere the whales still slide by, their spouts perpendicular, American elephants, remembering everything.

We are all going to the lost-and-found, he told them.

Accompanying him in what was like a marriage, Jasmin wept.